CITY OF CANNIBALS

City of Cannibals

RICKI THOMPSON

FRONT STREET
Honesdale, Pennsylvania

Library of Congress Cataloging-in-Publication Data

Thompson, Ricki.
City of cannibals / Ricki Thompson. — 1st ed.
p. cm.
Summary: In 1536 England, sixteen-year-old Dell runs away from her
brutal father and life in a cave carrying only a hand-made puppet to travel
to London, where she learns truths about her mother's death and the
conflict between King Henry VIII and the Catholic Church.
ISBN 978-1-59078-623-9 (hardcover : alk. paper)
[1. Runaways—Fiction. 2. Persecution—Fiction. 3. Monks—Fiction.
4. Puppet theater—Fiction. 5. London (England)—History—16th century—
Fiction. 6. Great Britain—History—Henry VIII, 1509-1547—Fiction.]
I. Title.
PZ7.T371987Cit 2010
[Fic]—dc22

2010002105

FRONT STREET
An Imprint of Boyds Mills Press, Inc.
815 Church Street
Honesdale, Pennsylvania 18431

10 9 8 7 6 5 4 3 2

To my family

CITY OF CANNIBALS

CHAPTER

I

Dell jolted upright. Something was out there.

She crawled around her brother, who lay curled under his blanket. Father's pallet was empty. She crept out of the cave.

Nothing. Only a log crumbling in the fire. And the restless shifting of the rabbits. Then a rustling sound. The Brown Boy, come to see her? She squinted into the darkness.

No, of course not. The Brown Boy *never* came this far up the mountain. A weasel, mayhap, prowling in the brush. She picked up a rock, threw it. Silence.

Black clouds tumbled across the thin white blade of the moon. Auntie's cottage and their half-built one rose, like specters, in the darkness. The skin on Dell's neck prickled.

Step, drag. Step, drag. Father. He was still a ways up the mountain, probably near the grotto. The rabbits scraped and scuffled in their hutch.

Step, drag. Father was stopping, at his usual place, to piss. Dell listened. His piss didn't shoot out in a single, direct stream. It splattered all over the rock and across the leaves of the buckthorn. He was drunk and would be a long time getting here. Dell unlatched the door of the rabbit hutch and reached inside to make sure the rabbits, especially Ezekiel, were safe.

Step, drag, step, drag. The footsteps were growing louder. Father was moving much faster than Dell had expected. Her trembling fingers fumbled to hook the latch. Why couldn't the footsteps belong to the Brown Boy? Why couldn't *he* be the one rushing down the path?

Before she could dash back to the cave, Father's shadowy bulk appeared beside it. A sour fear rose in Dell's throat. Even though Father was only half her height, his body was dense with muscle. And will.

Something limp dangled from his hand. A fish? She pressed her back against the hutch, barely breathing. A log flared, and Father's eyes met hers. The light from the fire illuminated the catch swinging in his hand.

"No!" she cried. "No!"

Father careened toward the fire.

"Not Eleanor!" She dove at him and grabbed Eleanor's arm. "Let go!" She was on her knees now, eye to eye with him, but Father held the puppet tight. Dell pulled harder, and the puppet's hand ripped off in hers. She fell back.

He spun Eleanor in the air—round and round—and then slammed her down, smashing her head on a stump. "The past is done," he growled.

Dell lunged at him, but her knees caught in her long woolen skirt and her arms scraped the ground. Father hurled Eleanor—what was left of her—into the flames.

The puppet's gown began to shrivel. As Dell scrambled

toward the fire, Father drew back his arm. He smashed his fist against her jaw, and it exploded with pain. Dell clutched at her face.

Father looked at his hand in surprise—as if it belonged to someone else—and then his squat, packed body pitched earthward. His tunic was inches from the fire, and Dell fought the urge to shove him into it, to make him burn like Eleanor.

He groaned and rolled onto his back. "You know what burns in those fires," he muttered. "You know." He began to snore.

Dell's jaw throbbed. What had roused her father to such fury? She found a stick and dragged Eleanor's remains out of the fire. The puppet's head was shattered, and her gown—the gown Dell had spent hours sewing—was nothing but ashy shreds. Dizzy with pain and confusion, Dell limped back to the cave.

Her brother still slept on his pallet, breathing out soft puffs of air. This was all his doing. He had spied on her. He had told Father where she hid her puppets. She yanked the thin spread off his body.

"Go away," he mumbled into the pallet.

She kicked his rump. "Tell me," she demanded. "Tell me why you gave him my puppet."

Nathaniel fumbled for the blanket. "I didn't," he whimpered. "Leave me alone."

Dell grabbed his arm and pulled him onto his side. "Tell me."

He twisted out of her grasp. "I was just looking at it.

And he came up on me. I swear."

"Liar."

He pulled the blanket over his head. "You should be glad he only got the girl."

She gave him one last shove. "You'll be sorry," she hissed.

She was wrong, of course. Nathaniel didn't have to be sorry. He hadn't grown tall and gangly like Dell. He looked like Father and Auntie. He belonged. He always would.

Dell went back outside to breathe the quiet night air, but Father's snores scraped through the stillness. *The past is done.* What did he mean? And what did her puppet have to do with the past?

She picked up the fragments of Eleanor's head. How carefully Dell had made it—first drying out the squash, then drawing on the puppet's features with a blackened twig. How painstakingly she'd made Eleanor's hair, gluing on strand after strand of yarn with sap.

At least she still had Bartholomew and her rabbit, Ezekiel. Tomorrow she would hide her other puppet in a new place where no one would find him. And Ezekiel would be around for a long time, eating and sleeping and mating. And of course she would always have the Brown Boy. Father could never steal *him* away.

The next morning, after prayers, Dell hurried to the hollow yew tree where she hid her puppets. She found Bartholomew just where she had left him, in the base of the tree under a pile of dry leaves. She smoothed out his harlequin suit and propped him against the trunk.

"I have sorrowful news," she said. "Father destroyed Eleanor last night, and we must bury her remains. And quickly. Before he finds us."

Bartholomew's head flopped over onto his chest, so Dell piled rocks around him to hold him up. He watched, silent, as Dell pulled up a handful of grass and began to break up the loose soil. She understood the sadness Bartholomew must be feeling. Dell had lost someone too—someone much dearer than Eleanor. Dell's mother was buried on this mountain. She lay in the earth, beneath the wooden cross. Silent and alone.

Dell dug more furiously now, scraping out dirt and rocks until her knuckles were encrusted with soil and blood. When the hole was deep enough, she laid Eleanor's remains inside and patted the earth back in place.

"Ashes to ashes," she said. She dusted off Bartholomew's suit and slipped him on her hand.

Bartholomew picked a sprig of violets and laid it on the grave. "Dust to dust."

Footsteps thudded up the path, and Bartholomew's harlequin suit began to quake. "Don't just stand there!" he sputtered.

Dell jammed him into her pocket and whirled around. Nathaniel strode toward her, a pail swinging from his hand.

She nodded at the pail and spoke in her calmest voice. "Shall we harvest the watercress together, the way we used to?"

As she knelt beside her brother and dipped her hands into the chilly current, she recalled earlier, happier moments—times before she and Nathaniel had sprouted their woman and man-fur. Days when Nathaniel still boasted how he would surpass Dell in height and strength, how he would become her protector. But now he was often angry at Dell, as if she and her unceasing growth had somehow betrayed him.

"Father says a girl of sixteen is too old to play with dolls."

"He's not a doll," Dell said, yanking out a clump of watercress. Bartholomew was something more—she was sure of it—but she didn't know what.

Nathaniel grabbed a bunch of watercress closer to shore. "Father will have your little man sooner or later. You know he will."

After they filled the pail, Dell pocketed a few sprigs to give to the rabbits. They loved the bitter herb almost as much as Auntie. At the hutch Dell unfastened the latch, laid down fresh grass, and set a bowl of clean water inside. She loved all four of the rabbits, but she especially loved Ezekiel. He hopped toward the bowl and gave it a shove. Water sploshed over the top. Dell offered him the watercress, but he turned his back on that, too. Dell smiled. He wanted something more, and he wanted it now.

He pushed his nose through the wooden slats, his whiskers tickling her fingers.

Dell glanced around—she'd been warned not to play with the rabbits—then grabbed the loose fold of skin behind Ezekiel's ears. His toenails grazed the wood as she dragged him out. Even though he loved to be held, he always resisted leaving the security of his hutch.

He squirmed for a moment, then settled in her arms, working his nose into the dark warmth of her armpit. With one finger she stroked behind his ears, where his fur grew deep and white and softer than down. His rapid heartbeat began to slow. He sniffed the bodice of her smock.

On a rock by the fire ring lay the first bunch of spring carrots, washed and ready to add to the supper pot. She moved, step by step, toward the carrots. If she took the puniest one, maybe no one would notice.

She had just whisked it up when Nathaniel stomped out of the bushes. Dell stuffed the carrot into her bodice, but it was too late. He'd seen everything. He'd become like a spoorne or a hobgoblin lately, watching her. He tossed one, then two pinecones into the air and began juggling them. Maybe he just wanted to perform for her, the way he used to—before Father had caught him somersaulting over the woodpile and thrashed him for it.

She held Ezekiel close. "Why aren't you checking the traps?"

"They're empty. Three days now." He stopped juggling, and as the pinecones fell earthward, he kicked one at Dell. "Father says we'll eat rabbit stew soon."

The pinecone pinged off Ezekiel's haunch, and she

turned sideways to protect him. "That's not true. Father keeps the rabbits for mating, not for eating."

Nathaniel withdrew two more pinecones from his pocket. "Watch me. I can juggle three."

"If Father catches you juggling again, you're in for it. It reminds him."

The pinecones moved around Nathaniel's head in a smooth, effortless arc. "No," he said. "What reminds him now is *you*."

Dell sat with her family by the fire, eating supper. Even Father's sullenness could not quell the excitement stirring inside her. Tonight the moon would wane to its slenderest self, which meant that tomorrow she would get to go down the mountain to the Boy.

Nathaniel stood by the fire, poking at the logs with a stick. Auntie grabbed it out of his hand. "Sit," she said. "Eat."

Father licked the rim of the wooden bowl. Dell hopped up and reached for the iron ladle in the pot. "More, Father?" She didn't want to displease him—not tonight.

He held out his bowl but did not look at her. "The contents of the sack are none of your business."

"I know, Father."

Nathaniel thrust his bowl at her, too. Even though he was only thirteen—three whole years younger than Dell—he was treating her as if *she* were the child. She ladled pottage into his bowl, purposely spilling some of the hot sauce onto his wrist. He jerked back, and for a moment she regretted her unkindness.

Father slurped at the pottage. "You will not show yourself to the boy."

"Yes. I mean, I won't, Father."

"Or venture past your mother's cross." He gripped his spoon as if it were a knife. "You know why it is called the City of Cannibals."

Dell nodded.

"And you must carry the sack with special care," Auntie added. "Mayhap it will contain lemons."

Dell dropped the ladle into the pot. "Lemons?" she cried. "Truly?"

"Why can't *I* go?" Nathaniel said. "I'm stronger than she."

Dell's body stiffened. "He can't," she choked. "It's *my* job. The sack is too big for him."

Nathaniel drew himself up tall. "Is not."

"Next time," Father said.

Dell's stomach churned. She would leave early tomorrow. Before Father could change his mind.

CHAPTER

II

Dell rose before the rooster had even flapped his wings. She rolled up the empty sack that lay at the end of her pallet and tucked it under her arm. Today was her last chance to see the Brown Boy, and no one was going to stop her.

A white wisp of moon still hung in the black sky. She shivered. What would she have left without the Boy? Nathaniel had once been her friend, but now. ...

Bartholomew—he was a friend of sorts. But still, sometimes—like now—she yearned for something more. What *was* it? She had plenty of food to eat, a pallet to sleep on, and an extra pair of leggings. Why, she even had the Bible to read.

The morning chill quickened her step and she walked faster now, rubbing her hands together for warmth. Maybe *that's* what she wanted. The touch of a hand. Not a puppet hand, but a *real* hand—like the Boy's. And if it was calloused or dirty or even bleeding—she didn't care—just so long as it was his.

She walked and prayed and listened for the sounds of morning. At last a lark sang out, and night began to melt away. In the muted, predawn light, Father and Auntie began to dissolve, too. By the time dawn broke, they were distant shadows.

Now that she could see the path, Dell could move even faster, skimming over rocks and roots and grasses bright with dew. The stream rushed along beside her, babbling its morning litanies of joy and good cheer. "Soon," it burbled. "Soon."

Sparrows chittered and robins trilled. By the time she arrived at the wooden cross, she was damp with sweat. Her curly black hair stuck to her neck, and dust coated her lips. She lay sprigs of violets and rue around her mother's grave and set down the empty sack where the Boy would find it and take it back down the mountain.

Dell tried to imagine what her mother had looked like when she had been a lady-in-waiting for Queen Catherine. Had Lucretia worn violet dresses to match her violet eyes? Or mayhap ivory gowns, to set off her raven hair? She had been modest and virtuous, Auntie had told Dell that much. No wonder King Henry had taken note of Lucretia.

Dusty and dirty from the long walk, Dell scrambled to the stream, dipped in her hands, and splashed water on her face. The water swirled brownish, and then the current swept the stream clean as it rushed down the mountain to the city below.

She leaned over a clear pool near the bank, and from the water's stillness a pair of inquiring eyes looked up at her. Violet eyes, like her mother's. Dell reached down to touch the face in the water, but a school of minnows darted past, shattering the image, scattering it across the quiet pool. She scooped water in her hands to drink and then, just in case the Boy came early, hurried to her hiding place.

She scrambled over the trunk of the fallen fir tree and crouched behind its roots. High winds—or maybe time—had yanked the huge tree out of the earth and laid it flat. The sticking-out roots had formed a loose and tangled web taller than Dell and twice the span of any other fir. Some of the roots were thick as branches, while others were short and threadlike. Among the tangles were open spaces through which she could watch. Even though she was only a hundred paces from the cross, the Boy would not be able to see her.

He might not come for hours—the journey up the mountain was long—but he *would* come—he was as unfailing as the waning moon. He would come to the wooden cross. To her. To Dell. She watched and waited. From her place behind the roots, she could see the last two turns of the path.

The cross marked the site where Dell's mother, Lucretia, was buried. On it Father had carved her name and the year of her death. MDXXIV. 1524. But the cross also stood as a warning. *Stop!* it said. *Do not venture farther. Everything beyond this spot is dangerous and tainted with the unpardonable sins of the city.*

Dell took Bartholomew from her pocket and slipped him on her hand. He gave his head an indignant shake. "It's about time you allowed me out of that dark hole."

She passed the time by telling him stories about the Boy—how he would find her crouching behind the fir tree and take her by the hand and lead her through the tangle of roots to the stream. His hand would be calloused from holding the rope that tied the sack, and dirty from the long walk up the mountain. Dell looked at her own hand. It was dirty and calloused, too, just like the Boy's. Bartholomew's head nodded.

At last a sound—the crumble of loose rocks being crunched underfoot—came from the path. Dell leapt to her feet. The Boy! He bobbed around the turn in the path, then stopped. Dell scrambled up on a thick root to get a better look. He slid the huge sack off his back, threw back the hood of his tunic, and grinned.

It drove her mad—that grin of his. She wanted to run down the path right now and ask him what made him smile like that, at absolutely nothing. But of course she didn't. There would be trouble, Father had warned her, if she did. She peered out over the knot of roots.

The Boy was so different from Father and Nathaniel. For one thing, his clothing was different. Instead of leggings and a short tunic, he wore a long black one—the kind peculiar to priests and monks. Auntie had told Dell all about holy men who dedicated their lives to God and lived in monasteries. The Brown Boy couldn't be a monk, she was certain. A monk didn't climb mountains and call out in a voice so loud, it echoed off the rocks. No, monks prayed and fasted and sometimes even took vows of silence.

The Boy, unlike Father and Nathaniel, was uncommonly tall, and when she watched his long-legged strides up the mountain, she felt a kinship with him. Did he, like Dell, suffer the rejection of his family? Was that why he brought the sack up the mountain—to escape his family's ridicule? Or was he an accepted part of something—like one of the twelve disciples of Jesus? Well, whatever the Boy's lot, he seemed to have accepted it with a glad and cheerful heart.

That was what fixed her gaze on him—his cheerful heart. She couldn't actually see it, of course, but its puzzling gladness glowed on his skin, turned up the corners of his lips, and sparked in his eyes. Like right now, there he was, grinning up at the empty sky as if it were a bowl of sugared treats. No one at home smiled the way he did. She and Nathaniel used to laugh together, but not anymore. Father mostly sneered now, and Auntie's lips quivered a little when she prayed. Maybe once, long ago, her mother had smiled enough for them all.

If she came close enough to the Boy, perhaps a tiny spark would leap from his heart into hers and warm her with its joy. She flushed at the foolish thought. Joy wasn't real—it was just a word in Auntie's Bible. But a smile—just one smile from the Boy—would keep her warm for a hundred years.

He shaded his eyes and looked directly at the fir tree. Dell clutched at a root and held her breath. His gaze seemed to penetrate the tangle, as if his eyes were looking right into hers.

The Boy cupped his hands around his mouth. "Good morrow," he called out.

"Morrow," the hillside echoed.

Every time the Boy came here, he shouted *good morrow*—as if he were calling out to her. How she longed to call back—especially today. She smoothed her white bodice, brushed the dirt from her blue skirt.

The Brown Boy bent over and grabbed the neck of the bulging sack and threw it over his shoulder as if it were a catch of fish. He had to round just one more bend in the path before he arrived at the cross.

She had named him the Brown Boy because he had brown hair and brown eyes and skin that shone as brown as an acorn at summer's end. He seemed a bit older than she— and at least a head taller. If his voice had a color, it would be brown, too—not the pale dun of her brother's voice, but a rich, deep hue—the color of rain-drenched soil.

Dell pulled back her black tangle of hair and twisted it into a makeshift braid. The Boy's hair was smooth and short and so orderly, it looked like a wooden bowl on top of his brown head. Only his nose lacked smoothness. It was crooked, probably broken in a fight with the cannibals.

When he finally arrived at the wooden cross, he set down the sack with a grunt and disappeared into the trees. Mayhap to relieve himself. Dell stood on her toes and strained to see into the foliage. Why he needed to be modest when he was so far away from the eyes of other people, she couldn't imagine.

When he returned, he knelt and laid a crocus at the foot of the cross, beside Dell's violets. "Lo," he said. "The winter is past, the rain is over and gone; the flowers appear on the earth."

Dell stifled a gasp. He was quoting from *The Song of Solomon*. She knew that book of the Bible by heart, too, every verse.

He continued his recitation in a loud voice. "O, my dove, that art in the clefts of the rocks, let me see thy countenance, let me hear thy voice."

Dell fingered the neck of her smock. If only he was calling out to her. If only she could answer him. Instead she whispered a verse back, but so softly only Bartholomew could hear. "Sweet is thy voice, and thy countenance is comely."

Bartholomew covered his ears. "Drivel," he muttered.

She waited for the Boy to say more, but he simply sighed and leaned against the cross. He unplugged his leather flask and brought it to his lips. Dell couldn't see if the flask contained water or blood, but the bun he took from his satchel was certainly not made of human flesh. It was an ordinary brown bun. Her stomach grumbled. If she hadn't been in such a hurry this morning, she would have brought along something to eat.

The Boy tore a chunk off his bun and chewed. Dell's mouth watered. She was starving. After he had swallowed every bite, he wiped his lips and stretched out on a sun-warmed patch of earth beside the cross. He laced his hands behind his smooth brown hair and closed his eyes. Even in sleep, the Boy's confounding smile remained fixed on his face. His black tunic rose and fell as he breathed, rose and fell.

She could go to him right now, while he slept, and kneel beside him. She could touch a strand of that smooth straight hair, smell his brown skin, stroke the hem of his rough tunic. It might be her last chance.

High above the boy, the branch of a larch tree rustled. A squirrel. It scrabbled down the trunk, leapt to the ground, and rose up on its haunches. Its quivering nose pointed at the lip of the sack. *Her* sack. The sack that might contain lemons.

The willful creature darted past the sleeping Boy, dashed up the side of the sack, and sat atop it, like a king on his throne. How dare it! Furious, Dell grabbed a clod of dirt and flung it, as hard as she could, at the squirrel. *Thunk.* The clod hit the Boy right on his cap of smooth brown hair.

He sat upright, and the squirrel scrambled back up the tree. The Boy rubbed his head. "Halloo?" he called out. Dell held her breath. The squirrel leaned down over its branch and chittered angrily.

The Boy looked up. "Aha," he said to the squirrel. "It was you, you troublemaker." He withdrew another bun from his satchel, tore it apart, and laid half of it at the base of the tree. "Here you are, my friend. I have enough for two."

Jealousy stung Dell. The boy had spoken to that miserable, complaining creature, had even broken bread with it.

And all the while she had remained hidden behind a tree, starving.

The Boy shook the dirt out of his hair and quoted from *The Song of Solomon* again. "Arise, my love, my fair one, and come away."

Dell pressed her breasts against the knot of roots. His words seemed to dare her to run into the open. She crushed a clod of dirt in her fist. He was leaving, she would never see him again and—she realized with a jolt—she didn't even know his name. He tipped his head in the direction of her tree. "Until next time," he called out.

Next time? Ha! There would be no next time. "Don't go," she whispered. She wanted time to memorize him, to paint the image of him in her mind's eye, to form the imprint of his hand over hers. "Not yet." He picked up the empty sack Dell had laid beside the cross for him, and then he turned to go.

Without the full sack over his shoulder, the Brown Boy moved quickly and lightly along the path. He rounded the first bend, and then the second, and in a moment he was lost to her, swallowed up by the forbidden world that lay below.

CHAPTER

III

Dell kicked at the dirt and roots until clouds of dust rose up, filling her mouth and eyes with grit. The Boy was gone. Gone, gone, *gone*.

At least she had the sack. The squirrel flicked its tail and inched its way down the tree, creeping closer and closer to the bun the Boy had set on the ground.

"Thief!" she shouted. She grabbed up a handful of pebbles and threw them as hard as she could. As the squirrel skittered away, Dell ran out and snatched the bun. Her throat felt thick and dry, but she stuffed the bread in her mouth and choked down every crumb.

The sack, of course, was none of her business. *A good beating, girl! That's what will come of prying in other people's business.* But Auntie had said that the sack might contain lemons. And if Dell couldn't have the Boy, she at least deserved a lemon. She drew her finger along the coarse fabric of the sack, imagining that she was touching the hem of his tunic.

The tip of a long angular object poked through the coarse weave. Mayhap a mattock for digging the garden, or a tool to spread daub on the wattle of their half-built cottage. She pressed a finger into one of the softer lumps and licked her lips. Probably almond paste. Or a gingerbread husband.

She picked at the knot that pinched the sack closed, wriggling the thick rope until the knot loosened. Nothing in Auntie's Bible had taught that *smelling* was a sin. She leaned her nose into the tiny opening she had created.

Ugh! The foul smell of goose grease and ash—soap—assaulted her. A harsh laugh broke the quiet, and she whirled around. A crow. Was it cautioning her to be obedient and good—like her mother?

Well, hang it all. Dell yanked off the rope, flung it aside, and dug both her hands into the sack. She pulled out two leather shoes and a pair of short woolen stockings.

She reached deeper and pulled out a rolled up bundle tied with a string. Her hands trembled as she untied it. The bundle unrolled all the way down to her ankles. A chemise. A new linen chemise to wear under her smock and skirt. And it looked as if it had been sewn just for her. If it had been made for Auntie, it wouldn't be half this long. And so clean and white! She held it up to her shoulders and smoothed it down over her skirt. Behind her a twig snapped and she whirled around. The squirrel condemned her—*chee-chee-chee*—from its high branch.

She dug her hand inside the sack again, wriggling it deeper and deeper. Raisins and prunes, quinces and currants. And could it be? Had they arrived at last, after so many months of waiting? Yes. She was almost certain. Here, beneath the pretzels and bags of seeds. She wrapped her fingers around one, lifted it, and held it up to the sun.

At last. She nested the lemon in her hands, cupped it, rolled it over and over, her own chafed skin rubbing on the skin of the lemon, skin pocked and smooth at the same time, the one tip of the lemon hard, like her teats when she bathed in the icy stream, the other tip sharp and rough where it had been plucked from its nourishing bough.

The lemon had its imperfections, of course. A splotch of brown here, two more of green there. She held the lemon under her nostrils and breathed. A cloud floated across the sun and left her standing in a chilly shadow. If she didn't start up the mountain now, she would have to drag the heavy sack in the dark, with only a thin blade of moon to light her way.

She bent down to get the rope but—shame on her!— she picked up a small pointed twig instead. Had the devil placed it here for her temptation? She glanced up into the tree—surely the squirrel would admonish her—but the creature was nowhere in sight. Good riddance, too. Not even Bartholomew could rebuke her now—he was sequestered in her pocket.

Time to go. But the twig. She pressed the point of it against the lemon and pushed it through the thick yellow skin. A tiny dewdrop of juice oozed out. Dell inhaled. Its scent was so clean, for a moment she felt as if she were a shaft of sunlight, pure, transparent.

She licked off the drop of juice. The sourness radiated along her tongue, across her lips, down her throat. She winced. The tang brought her to attention, awakened her. And somehow comforted her. Not the way a drop of sweet warm milk teased from their goat's udder comforted her. Some other kind of comfort she couldn't explain.

If Father saw the hole she'd made he would beat her with a stick. Only one thing to do. She dropped the lemon into her pocket.

Just as she leaned over to tie the sack, something sprang from its depths and shot into the air. Dell screamed. But it was only the squirrel—not a punishing demon—dragging a pretzel in its jaws.

"Shame on you," Dell cried. "Shame." But thank Heaven it wasn't an evil spirit. Or a cannibal. Just an ill-mannered squirrel. She tied the sack and heaved it over her shoulder. Stumbling under its weight, she headed up the path.

The next afternoon, after Dell had cleaned the rabbit hutch, she went to the wooden trough outside Auntie's cottage to wash her hands. The cottage wasn't much bigger than their cave, but the cottage had dry walls and a thatched roof and a window. Dell and Nathaniel and Father had a cottage too, but it had never been finished. The frame stood, like a ring of picked bones, beside the chestnut tree. Dell scrubbed her hands hard, careful to remove every speck of dirt from her knuckles and every trace of rabbit fur from her fingernails. There.

She entered the cottage and opened the shutters. Sunlight poured into the room, illuminating Auntie, straight-backed on her stool, crushing herbs with her mortar and pestle. Her hair was drawn back so tightly it stretched her eyes into the shape of almonds. She squinted at the sudden brightness. On the floor beside her sat a lemon. It had been sliced in half and its insides glistened.

"Your father suffers from catarrh again. We will make a remedy with lemon and herbs."

Dell's lemon lay, like a stolen treasure, in her pocket. She held out her hands, palms up, for Auntie to inspect. When she had examined every finger, Dell turned her hands palms down.

"You must never touch the Bible with dirty hands."

"No, Auntie."

"And if aught happens to that harlequin marker, your father will—"

"I know, Auntie." Dell picked up the sacred book. She ran her fingers over the black velvet cover and traced the words *Holy Bible* that were embroidered on it with golden threads. Inside the cover was scripted in pen, *To Lucretia from Catherine of Aragon MDXX*. 1520—sixteen years ago—the year Dell had been born.

"Was she kind—Queen Catherine?"

Auntie's eyes narrowed. "She taught your mother to read, did she not?"

"Tell me about their life at court," Dell ventured.

"I have told you everything. Your father was an entertainer, your mother rose to the position of lady-in-waiting."

"But they left the palace. Under cover of night." Dell paused. Maybe Auntie would drop her guard and fill in the blank spaces of her parents' past.

"Your mother was a beautiful woman." Auntie began to chew slowly, like she always did, even though her mouth was empty. "But virtuous. And King Henry was—*is* I daresay—a man of boundless appetite."

"And?"

"You goad me." Auntie pointed to the straw-filled mattress folded against the wall. "Sit."

Hugging the Bible, Dell moved toward the door, where there was more light.

"You shan't take the Bible out-of-doors."

"I'm not." Dell opened the book to the page where the strip of harlequin fabric lay, marking their place. Whenever she read out loud to the family, Father would press it to his cheek, or wind it round and round his fingers.

She stroked it—first the yellow square, then the green one, then the blue and the red. She loved the harlequin pattern so much, she'd sewn Bartholomew's costume in imitation of it. But unlike the stitches on this piece of fabric, Dell's stitches were clumsy and uneven. And Bartholomew's harlequin suit was made of wool and linen castoffs, not the fine silk and satin and velvet of this piece. This cloth was ragged along its borders, clearly ripped from a larger piece.

"Well?" Auntie said.

With a jerk of her head, Dell shook off her thoughts. She licked the tip of her finger and used it to turn the page.

"A book," said Auntie, "is no place for a girl's spittle."

"We were reading from Proverbs, chapter twenty-three," Dell said.

"Pay heed to the instruction of the Lord our God."

Dell draped the harlequin fabric over her wrist and began reading. "Who is the man who always has sorrows? Who is the man with red eyes? It is he who tarries with wine. Wine bites like a serpent. It stings like an adder. The drunkard—"

"The *drunkard*, you say?" Auntie's eyebrows came together into thin black clouds. "What right have you to criticize your father's habits?"

"I wasn't." Dell clutched the Bible to her breast. "I was—"

"He helped your mother to escape the palace. He thought she was safe. How could he have known?"

"Auntie, I was only reading the words of Proverbs."

"You don't know the bodily pains your father—and I—endure." Auntie rose from her stool. "You never will. You—who have never known pain—who are you to say his drinking is wrong?"

Dell rubbed the harlequin cloth. *Velvet, satin, silk.* If she was silent and waited, Auntie's fury would pass. *Velvet, satin, silk.*

"How dare you condemn him," Auntie said, "when it is you—you—"

Dell squeezed the cloth. The room grew small and dark.

Auntie pointed her finger at Dell. "How dare you—when it is *you* who are the cause of his suffering."

"Me?" What had Dell ever done to drive her father to drink?

Auntie's hand shook, and the pestle rattled in the bowl. "You remind him. Not only your violet eyes and your black curls, but—" She looked Dell up and down—from her thick mop of hair, over the bodice of her smock, past her blue woolen skirt, all the way down to her thin leather shoes. "everything about you reminds him of her."

Dell dropped the Bible on the wooden chest, and the harlequin marker fluttered to the floor. "*Everything*? You mean my mother was tall, like me? Why didn't you tell me? *Why?*"

"One question breeds another." Although Auntie's words were still sharp, the bitterness had drained from her voice. She began to grind the pestle into the bowl again, her wrist turning in a steady, rhythmic motion. "Pick up the cloth and put the Bible away. Your father's cloak needs mending."

CHAPTER
IV

Dell's needle was dull, and Father's cloak was thick. Her fingers throbbed. Anger and frustration welled in her, and she glared at Auntie. "Why did Mother and Father escape from the palace? Where did they go? How did they live?"

"I've told you. Their circumstances were much reduced. It was the will of God."

Dell jammed the needle through the fabric, right into her thumb. She cried out, but another sound—a shrill scream—made her jump. The skin rose on her neck, and she flung down the cloak. The scream came from an animal that was small—smaller than a fox.

It squealed again, and a hot pain shot through her. The scream sounded almost childlike. The death cry of a rabbit. Praise God it wasn't Ezekiel. She had just fed the rabbits an hour ago and had latched their door. Another scream.

Some predator had caught a rabbit right outside the cottage. But that wasn't possible. Wild animals never ventured so close in broad daylight. Unless the predator wasn't a wild animal. Unless …

"No!" Dell cried. She bolted outside.

Father stood by the fire, his legs spread, a bloody knife in one hand. In the other hand he held Ezekiel by his hind legs. The rabbit jerked and quivered, struggling to right himself, his eyes bulging in terror. For a moment Dell stood rooted to the ground, too stunned to move.

Ezekiel had been sliced open from his throat all the way to his tail. His belly was a mass of bloody innards. On the ground below him knelt Nathaniel, catching the blood in a pail. Ezekiel squealed once more, and his scream ripped through Dell. He was crying for help and she was helpless to save him. His body shuddered and went limp.

Dell ran at Father. "I hate you!" she screamed. She kicked the pail, and drops of blood splattered his shoes. "You promised they were for breeding."

Father shook Ezekiel in Dell's face. "This is dinner," he said. "And you will eat it." He motioned to Nathaniel. "Come, boy. It's time I showed you the tricks of cutting a perfect pelt." He limped toward the trees. "Clean up that mess," he called over his shoulder.

"Why didn't you break his neck first?" Dell shouted at his back. "Why did you make him suffer?"

Nathaniel grabbed Dell's sleeve. "I tried to stop him." He touched the dark welt rising on his cheek, then hurried after his father.

Dell sank to her knees and pushed handfuls of dust over the bright beads of Ezekiel's blood.

The cottage door slammed shut. "Honor thy father and thy mother," Auntie said. "Say it. Say it out loud."

Dell pushed Auntie's hand aside. "I have no mother."

Auntie grabbed hold of Dell's hair and jerked her to

her feet. Dell clenched her teeth—she would *not* give any sign of the pain she felt. Auntie marched toward the grotto, clinging tightly to Dell's hair, forcing her to stumble along in a stooped and twisted manner.

"Kneel," Auntie commanded when they arrived at the grotto, "and do penance for your sin." She pushed Dell's head down and marched away.

Dell raised her head. The sharp pebbles on the ground poked through her woolen skirt and leggings, and she shifted from one knee to the other.

After awhile the moon rose, pale and thin. A dull ache spread up her legs and across her back. Father had destroyed Eleanor and killed Ezekiel. Sooner or later he would destroy Bartholomew, too. If Dell stayed here, would she become dry and brittle like Auntie? Or like Father, sullen and bitter? She took out her puppet and slipped him on her hand. "Bartholomew," she said, "we can't stay here any longer."

"But there's no place to go," he said, "except the City of Cannibals."

"We'll find the Brown Boy."

"The Brown Boy! And what will he do? Fight off the cannibals? Are you mad?" Before he could say another word, she stuffed him in her pocket and hurried back to the cave. Her family had gone to bed, but a few embers still burned in the gray ash of the fire.

The three remaining rabbits scrabbled about in the hutch. Father had killed Ezekiel slowly, cruelly, and he would do the same to the others, too. She could release them now—give them a chance—while Father slept. Of course they might not survive the night. The badger and weasel were out there, waiting. Her heart thudded.

From inside the cave came the sound of Father's snoring. "Murderer," he muttered in his sleep. "Murderous devil." Who was he mumbling about? Himself? Somewhere in the distance an owl hooted, and its mate *whooed* back.

She paused between the fire ring and the hutch. A blackened log collapsed into the bed of ash, and red hot embers sparkled like hidden jewels. She thought again of Ezekiel—how she had looked on, helpless, while he died. Her hands shook as she unfastened the latch of the hutch. She grabbed one rabbit by the nape of its neck and carried it, squirming, into the alders. She hurried back for the other two. "May God protect you from the weasel," she whispered.

And then they were gone, and the brush was silent.

At least Dell still had Bartholomew. She would wear him like a glove, and he would talk to her while she traveled down the mountain. She wasn't a child—she knew he wasn't real. But a play toy? No, he was more than that. She slipped her hands into her pockets. In her left one lay her puppet, and in her right the lemon.

And far below her lay the city. *Do not be deceived*, Father had warned her. *Why do you think it is called the City of Cannibals? Because the people eat each other's flesh, they drink each other's blood.*

If Dell dared to enter the city, she might be sliced and

skinned like Ezekiel. If she stayed here, she could still make amends. And she could wear the new linen chemise that had come in the sack. Then she thought about Ezekiel's limp body, and about Eleanor's charred remains, and about who she would become if she remained on the mountain. No. Staying here wasn't the answer.

She walked for a long time down the path. Beside her the stream babbled psalms of consolation and hope. At last she arrived at Lucretia's wooden cross. The farthest down the mountain she had ever traveled. She took Bartholomew from her pocket and slipped him on her hand.

"I'm sore and weary," she said. "Shall we rest here?"

Bartholomew eyed Lucretia's grave. "I hope you speak of a temporal rest, not an eternal one."

"Did you think I had given up so quickly?" Dell plopped down on the patch of dirt where the Brown Boy had sat. She leaned wearily against the cross. It comforted her, somehow, sharing the same earth as the boy and being supported by Lucretia's cross. "Auntie says my mother died quickly."

"A blessing. To be crushed beneath a heavy booth would be a painful death."

"Such a dreadful mishap—the way the soldier lost control of his horse, and it reared up, and—"

"A mishap?" He shook his head. "How could it be? A king's soldier unskilled in the art of horsemanship?"

"I have forgiven the soldier for his fatal blunder. I pray an *ave* for him every day."

Bartholomew crossed his arms over his chest. "*I* pray that the wretch lost his post."

"And an *ave* for his horse also."

"*I* pray that the horse was made into stew meat and served to the king for supper."

"Do you think I am like Lucretia, as Auntie says?"

Bartholomew's painted smile seemed to grow larger. "You mean virtuous, modest, graceful, witty, devout, kind, obedient. ..."

She gave him a swat on his head. "I mean my bodily traits—my height, my curly black hair, my violet—" She opened her eyes as wide as she could and stared hard into Bartholomew's. "Do you think they are *haunting,* like my mother's?"

He drew close to her face. "I think they are open, and would be better closed."

A mouse, or maybe a vole skittered across Dell's skirt, and she startled.

"I will keep watch," Bartholomew said, "while you sleep."

She shut her eyes but slept restlessly, starting at every rustling in the brush. The black shroud of sky would be a perfect shelter for demons and hobgoblins.

A scream jolted Dell awake. Her body was soaked in sweat. The nightmare had come again, and the scream was her own. She shook her head, trying to dispel the images that assailed her.

The man in the red vest juggling lemons. Lemons

spinning higher and higher. The whinny of a horse. The scream.

If the Boy were here he would stroke her hand, wipe the beads of sweat from her brow. She drew Bartholomew close and he lay beside her, his eyes wide open but his head drooping on his chest.

The busy chitter of wrens told Dell that she had survived the night. Her hipbones ached where they had pressed against the rocky crust of earth. Her smock was moist with sweat, her woolen skirt damp with dew.

The dream clung to her like a sticky spider web. What did it mean—the man in the red vest juggling lemons? Maybe the Brown Boy could explain. After all, he was the one who came up the mountain carrying lemons. And a chemise that was just the right size for her too-tall body.

After she had washed her hands in the stream, she pulled Bartholomew from her pocket and slipped him on her hand. "Do you think Father will pursue me down the mountain?"

Bartholomew shook his head. "Even if he tries, he is ill and his legs pain him."

Dell looked down the mountain. Tendrils of smoke curled up from the city. "Father says that human flesh burns in those fires."

"Or perhaps the breakfast porridge."

"The Brown Boy will know."

Bartholomew crossed his arms over his chest. "Nonsense. The Brown Boy has no knowledge of you. Every time he comes up the mountain, you scurry behind the fir tree and whisper words of love to the pillbugs and beetles burrowing in its roots."

She gave him a shake. "Those words of love, I'll have you know, were from the *Song of Solomon*. But what would a hollowed-out squash know about love?"

"Love? Who said anything about—" But before he could utter another word, Dell thrust him in her pocket.

She scanned the mountain below her, searching for little clouds of dust made by hurrying feet. Maybe, by some miracle, the Boy would return to her and show her the way. But the path was quiet and empty. She would have to make this journey alone.

The path began to veer away from the stream, so Dell took one last draught of the cold, clear water. If only she had thought to bring a flask. After awhile the friendly burble of the stream faded. But grasshoppers still chirruped in the grasses, bluebottle flies darted this way and that, and birds flitted about as if they had nothing to consider except song and sun. Far below, the wall of the city began to take shape.

As the sun rose higher, a midday hush fell over the mountainside. Either the cannibals had retreated inside the city walls or they were hiding in the trees, watching.

Dell reached her fingers inside her pocket and touched the lemon. Its bumpy skin and its nubby tips reassured her. In her other pocket lay Bartholomew, still and silent.

With every step she took, the wall of the city loomed taller. With every turn in the path, it stretched out wider and longer. And in front of the wall she could make out a blur of activity.

The land became flatter and more open now, providing her with fewer places to hide. At the snap of a twig, she jumped. At the crunch of a dry leaf, she dove behind a rock.

The blur of motion outside the walls became more distinct. It was a swarm of people and animals. From here, the people seemed as tall as she and the Brown Boy. She rubbed her eyes. Certainly she was deceived. A cart lumbered along a rutted road, then turned and disappeared into the open gate of the city.

Without cover, she was easy prey. She ran to a large oak, then dashed a little farther to the safety of a blackthorn bush. She knelt on the white petals that had fallen from its branches and tried to catch her breath. If she could make it to that outcropping of rock, and then to the gorse bush, she could dash from it into the city.

If the cannibals saw her, she wouldn't have a chance. She was nothing but a paltry girl with no means of defense. They would slit her throat the way Father had slit Ezekiel's and roast her on a spit and peel off all her skin and eat her meaty parts and throw her leg bones to the dogs. She ran to the rock and then the gorse bush.

But if she stayed here, she would die of starvation and thirst. The crows would peck out her eyes. The badger and weasel would fight for the choicest parts of her flesh. And she would never see the Boy. Thorns scraped her cheek.

Close to the gate sat a woman. Unlike the people around her, the woman was sitting perfectly still, the way Auntie did at prayer. Maybe the woman was a good Christian who would help Dell.

Rocks poked into her knees. Thorns pulled at her hair. She leapt to her feet, lifted up her heavy skirt, and ran toward the open gate.

CHAPTER

Terrified, Dell kept her eyes on the ground. She skirted around a bleating sheep and a skittish goat. She wended her way through a labyrinth of skirts and boots and wheels. The bright sun blinded her, and she stumbled and pitched to the ground. Her elbows stung.

When she looked up, the woman at the gate was staring down at her. Dell choked on a mouthful of dust. The woman's lips were twisted, and her filthy hair hung in tangled cords about her face. A terrible smell—like spoiled meat—hung in the air. Dell pushed herself to her knees, waving away the flies that encircled her.

The woman was not praying. Her arm was outstretched and her gnarled hand was upturned. Dell had read enough Bible stories to know that she was a beggar.

"Alms for a miserable soul," she whimpered. She smiled in a scornful way, and her teeth—what was left of them—were greenish, as if coated with moss. With a cackle, the woman lifted the hem of her ragged skirt. Her legs—which stopped at the knees—were two oozing stumps. Dell let out a gasp.

It was true, then. Someone—some cruel cannibal inside the city—had cut off this woman's legs and roasted them, like legs of mutton, on a spit.

"Alms," the woman whined again. She leaned forward, using one hand to support her weight. With her other hand, she snatched a handful of Dell's skirt.

Dell pulled back, but the woman only clung tighter. Dell dug into her pocket. Under the lemon lay a piece of carrot, left from Ezekiel's last meal. Well, she certainly wasn't going to give her lemon away. She thrust the carrot into the woman's hand. Instantly the beggar let go of Dell's skirt. The woman bit into the carrot with the few teeth she had left.

Dell felt sick, but she *had* to ask. "Will they kill me?" she said. "In the city?"

The woman chewed and swallowed. "Ashes to ashes. Dust to dust."

"And eat me as well?"

The woman sniggered and looked in the direction of the mountain. "You are like me," she said. As she spoke, bits of carrot sprayed from her mouth. "I disobeyed God, too. And look how He has punished me." She hitched up her skirt again, revealing the stumps of blackened flesh.

Bile rose in Dell's throat.

"If you continue in your evil ways, God will punish you, too." Somehow, despite her crippled legs, the woman lunged at Dell, who jumped to her feet and stumbled headfirst through the open gate. She threw herself to one side, pressing her back against the wall. If they were going to kill her, then quickly. She shut her eyes. Do it quickly.

She stood motionless until the damp chill of the stones seeped through her smock. A clattering din assaulted her, and a foul stew of smells made her belly churn. She slid down the sharp, chilly stones and crouched there, her hands over her face. One of the smells overpowered all the others. Stale piss.

Still crouching, she opened her eyes and took a deeper breath. The stench came from behind her. It was the wall. This was where the cannibals came to relieve themselves. She scuttled forward before the stench could seep into her smock. On the wall were splatters of dried blood and other stains she couldn't identify. She tucked her head between her knees and tried not to be sick.

An odor of roasting meat mingled with the other smells. She could *taste* them, as if the piss and meat and shit were a soup she had swallowed. Her chest tightened.

The lemon. She pulled it out of her pocket and pressed it to her nose. The scent of the lemon almost masked the stench. The fruit's nub felt like a chafed but tender finger brushing across her lip.

Carts rattled, pigs squealed, people shouted. But not one voice called out, *Roasted man-flesh here! Come and get your tasty child-meat here!*

"Hulla! Hulla!" a voice shouted. Dell looked up. A huge man stood high above her in a cart with big wheels. He raised a long stick over his head. The stick lashed back and forth like an angry snake. It sliced through the air, and the tip of it grazed Dell's shoulder. Oddly, she felt relieved by the stinging pain. It meant she was still alive. And Bartholomew. She felt for him through the fabric of her skirt. Yes, he was still safe, too.

She pushed the lemon into her pocket, staggered to her feet, and ran. But the ground was slippery, and her feet slid out from under her. She hit the street with a splat. Mud squelched under her hands. And oozing in between her fingers, along with the mud, were tiny fish bones and animal guts. The fetid slime sogged her skirt. She scrambled to her feet.

Where was the Boy?

A cloud of smoke filled the air in front of her and stung her eyes. Dripping fat sizzled, and through the greasy smoke, Dell could see something turning on a spit. It was a human leg—it was the leg of the woman who sat outside the gate. She looked closer. No. Not a human leg. A leg of mutton. Just mutton.

Father was right. This city was Hell, and now she was a part of it. Her eyes blurred with tears, but whether they were caused by remorse or smoke, she couldn't tell. She scurried around a corner so fast she bumped right into the hindquarters of an ass. A man held up the donkey's front foot, and a boy dug at it with a stick. The boy was hidden behind the donkey's flank, but his shoes—they looked just like the shoes of the Brown Boy.

"Boy!" Dell cried. The boy stood up straight and smiled behind the swayed back of the ass.

"Oh," she said. And then more quietly, "Oh."

The boy had no front teeth, and his eyeballs turned in, not out, so that he appeared to be smiling not at her, but at his own nose. His clothing was all wrong, too. He wore a short tunic and leggings, like Nathaniel, not the long black tunic of the Brown Boy.

The man scowled at the boy. "Goggling," he said, "won't get the stone from my ass's hoof."

Dell backed away. Even though the boy wasn't the Brown Boy, he was as tall as the Boy. Maybe even taller. The man beside him was tall also. She glanced around. The people to her right and left were tall. And the people behind her.

She stood there, gaping. She had been so dazed and terrified, she hadn't seen—really *seen*—anyone until this moment. Everyone around her had long arms and long legs and flat foreheads like hers. No one looked like Father or Auntie or Nathaniel. They were all as stretched-out as Dell. Did that mean that she was a cannibal, too, like the people here? No, no, Lucretia had been tall, and the Brown Boy also, and they weren't cannibals.

Above her, wooden signs creaked and swung in the breeze. The signs had pictures on them, and words as well. *Haberdasher. Tailor. Bladesmith.* She crept past a brazier of roasting nuts and a stack of caged linnets. No matter which direction she looked, she saw people. And all of them tall. They pushed and jostled and shouted. People, people, people.

She stayed close to buildings, her shoulder brushing the whitewashed walls. The sight of so many things all at once made her light-headed. Some of them—the crates and casks, the vendors and carts and buildings—she could identify from the many stories Auntie had told her. And the foods—

the onions and turnips and cabbages—she'd eaten those on the mountain. But other things—what *were* they?

They were strange ... and yet ... unsurprising, as if she'd experienced them in some other life—a life before her last twelve years on the mountain. Even the horrid smells seemed familiar. She pressed on.

Just beyond the next fire—a boar this time, just the haunch of a wild boar—a crowd had gathered. Men and women and children, too. The children jumped up and down, clapping their hands. Everyone was smiling, even laughing. Surely they wouldn't laugh if they were about to be killed. Dell stood at the edge of the crowd, straining to see.

Father and Auntie and Nathaniel never laughed anymore. Until this moment, laughter had been only in her heart. Now murmurs of pleasure and delight surrounded her. What could be causing so much gaiety? She wriggled into the center of the crowd, stood on her toes, craned her neck forward.

CHAPTER

VI

In front of the crowd rose a wooden booth—a big one—at least two heads taller than Dell and two arm spans wide. Its pretty blue curtain rippled in the breeze. She'd seen this booth—or one like it—before. But where? Across the front of the booth hung a sign:

THE JUDGEMENT OF KIT

She took Bartholomew from her pocket so he could see, too. "Remember what I told you about my mother's death?" she whispered to him. "How a royal horse reared up and crushed her inside a booth? I have a peculiar feeling that it was a booth like this one."

Bartholomew struggled to get a better look. "What is its purpose?"

Before Dell could answer, an ugly little man flew up in front of the curtain. Dell startled in surprise. He was a puppet, like Bartholomew. His furry eyebrows bristled out over his hooked nose, and his shiny black eyes looked angry. He banged on the stage with a club—*Clack! Clack! Clack!*—and up popped another puppet—a craggy-chinned woman wearing a close-fitting cap and an apron.

Bartholomew squirmed with excitement. "Performers!" he cried. "On a real stage! That is where *I* should be!"

Dell laid a hand over his mouth. She'd always wondered how she knew about puppets. Was it possible that her parents had become puppeteers after they had escaped from the palace? Not Father. His hands were too thick and stubby to fit in a puppet suit.

Had Lucretia taught Dell how to make puppets—how to hollow out the squash and sew tiny hands in the shape of mittens? Had Lucretia shown her how to fit her pointing finger into the puppet's neck, her thumb and third finger into the puppet's arms? It had to be. How else could Dell have known each and every detail of the craft?

Bartholomew tugged at Dell's sleeve and pointed to the stage.

"Vile husband!" screamed the woman puppet. "Wicked Kit!"

"Not I, but you, Polly," Kit growled, and swung the club at his wife. She ducked, then butted him with her craggy head. The laughter of the crowd dwindled to a few nervous titters.

"A pox on you!" Polly shrieked. "You drowned the baby!" Polly's cloth body shook. She raised her head and howled and then dropped out of sight. An instant later a third character leapt onto the stage. He had pointy red horns and a long red tail and a red cape. A murmur ran through the crowd.

"The devil," Dell cried.

"Who was you expecting?" the woman beside her muttered. "King Henry himself?"

The devil jabbed Kit with his spear. Kit dropped his club, and it clattered onto the stage. "Not I!" Kit wailed. He held out his arms in supplication to the audience, but the crowd only hissed at him. He banged his head on the stage. "Polly drowned the baby! 'Twas Polly!"

The devil roared. The crowd gasped. With his spear, Satan jabbed Kit again and again, pushing him down, down, down into the raging fires of Hell. The crowd applauded—a few threw coins into a hat—and then they drifted away.

Dell stepped closer to the booth. Yes, of course. Her mother—a puppeteer—crushed inside a booth like this one. Dell reached out her hand and ran one finger along the edge of the stage. And Father, dashing Eleanor's head against a rock. *The past is done*, he'd said. Did he think that by destroying the puppet, he could destroy his painful memories, too? He'd kept nothing to remind him of the past— only the scrap of harlequin fabric that lay in the Bible.

"Why didn't Father tell me?" Her voice grew louder. "I had a right to know."

"Mayhap your father fears that puppets will destroy you, as they did your mother," said Bartholomew.

"But it wasn't the *puppets* that killed my mother. It was the *horse*."

"It was the *soldier* who did not control his horse."

Dell glanced around. The crowd was giving her a wide

berth. Maybe she *was* mad—talking to Bartholomew in public.

A screech made her jump back from the booth.

There stood the devil, waving his spear at her. "Off with you, wench!"

Dell shrank back, but Bartholomew's suit quivered with excitement. "At last—in this performance—I have seen my future." He extended his arms in a grandiose gesture.

Dell rolled her eyes. But she had seen something, too. Not her future, but her past. *The past is done.* But was it?

"Well?" said Bartholomew.

"Mind your place," she said. "Remember—today you are just a hollowed-out squash in a faded harlequin suit."

"I may have the head of a squash, but you ... *you* are the thick-headed one. Can't you see that *I* am an actor? And that our destinies are linked?"

"Your destiny and mine? I will think on it, but first we must find the Brown Boy."

"The Brown Boy, the Brown Boy. Do you think only of your own desires? What of *me*, what of *my* desires?"

Dell stuffed Bartholomew in her pocket and moved on, weaving her way between carts and drays. Was all love like Kit's and Polly's—harsh and cruel? What about her own parents? Had Lucretia really loved Father? Had he once been a loving man, free of anger and meanness? Well, at least the Brown Boy wasn't cruel. He had even shared his bread with a lowly squirrel.

She turned down a narrow alley with fewer people and

no carts. For a moment she felt safer, but then a man beckoned to her from a doorway, curling his finger at her to come closer, and she fled back to the crowded street.

Around the next corner, the street opened onto a large grassy field that rose into a hill. Like the street, the hill was swarming with people—hundreds upon hundreds of them—but none of them appeared to be killing or eating one another. Nevertheless, Dell crouched behind a barrel and watched.

In the center of the crowd rose another stage. But this one stood high above the crowd, and it was built for people, not puppets, to walk across.

It was empty except for a block of wood the size of the stump she sat on at home. Perhaps a performer was coming to sit on it and tell a story. She wriggled into the crowd where no one would notice her. People pressed in on her so tightly, she could hardly breathe. She couldn't even reach into her pockets to touch Bartholomew or the lemon. Her puppet's head was sturdy and—God willing—would not be crushed.

Her head spun with the odors of human sweat and foul breath. But the most powerful smell of all was the odor of dead fish. Dell glanced in the direction of the stink. There, pressing against her arm, stood a girl about her own age.

Dell's mouth fell open. She had never been this close to a real girl. Her cheeks were plump but pale as cream, and tight russet curls stuck out from her cap. She was so close, she was breathing her fishy breath right on Dell's neck.

The girl stared up at the empty stage, and Dell stared at the girl. Her bosom pressed against Dell's arm. Dell looked down at her own scrawny body. Maybe, if she remained in the city, she would become plump and womanly, too. With one dirt-encrusted finger she touched the girl's sleeve.

"Don't be touching me," she said, jerking her shoulder away.

Dell wedged her hand back into her pocket. She wanted to say something, anything, but her tongue stuck like milkweed in her mouth. The girl squirmed away from her, past a burly man with a beard.

Dell squeezed around the man. "Girl," she said, before she even realized she had opened her mouth, "will there be songs?"

The girl gave Dell a little shove. "Get on," she said. "I aren't allowed to talk to no half-wits. Or whores."

"I am no half-wit," Dell said. But a whore? She knew about whores from the Bible, but wasn't quite sure which sins—or how many—made an ordinary woman a whore. "Please," she persisted, "what kind of show will it be?"

"You *do* be touched." The girl raised her nose in the air and looked down at Dell. "It be a execution," she said haughtily.

Dell had seen a drawing of an execution—Auntie had scraped one in the dirt with a stick. It was the outline of a dead man dangling from a noose. *The wages of sin is death*, Auntie had clucked. Dell shuddered. "But where are the gallows?"

"P-f-f-f-t," the girl spat. "John Fisher be a man of high rank, so he be getting the axe. The traitors of lesser rank—they *do* be hanged, and while they be yet alive—" The girl poked Dell's chin with her thumb, then drew it—like a knife—all the way along Dell's throat, between her breasts, down past her navel, down.

Dell pulled back, gasping for breath.

The girl gripped Dell's chin and continued. "Those traitors be cut up the middle, that's what. Now *that* be a fine show. Finer than—"

The sound of a trumpet interrupted the girl's speech.

The trumpeter—a man in shiny boots and a short red coat—clumped across the platform. He blew into the trumpet again. The sound blasted out over the din of the crowd.

The girl beside her knew everything. Surely she would know about cannibals. "After the execution," Dell said, "will you eat the dead man?"

"Eat him?" the girl cried out. "Like savages?"

Before she could say another word, three more men climbed onto the platform. The one in the center looked haggard and unshaven. On either side of him stood a guard—or maybe they were soldiers. How different they looked from the unkempt man between them—in their white leggings and scarlet tunics and their sleeves that puffed out like clouds. Each guard carried a sword and a halberd that was longer than they were tall. The elderly man in the center was singing the *Te Deum*. He stumbled on the steps, and the guards steadied him.

One more man clumped up to the stage. He wore a close-fitting scarlet robe, a scarlet mask, and a horn-shaped hat. He carried the biggest axe Dell had ever seen. Her chin quivered.

The crowd quieted, and the trumpet blower spoke. "By the royal command of his majesty, King Henry VIII, on this twenty-eighth day of April, the year of our Lord 1536, Bishop John Fisher, accused of …"

The traitor was a *bishop*? But that wasn't possible. Auntie had schooled Dell in all matters of religion, and she knew that a bishop was a man of authority in the church—higher even than a priest. "But—this Bishop Fisher—is he not a holy man of God?"

The girl grabbed Dell's ear and yanked it close. "S-s-s-s-t," she hissed, spraying her fishy spittle in Dell's face. "John Fisher be saying that the king had no the right to divorce Queen Catherine. He be saying only the Pope gots the right to give out divorces."

"Catherine of Aragon?" Dell said. "The queen?" Dell thought of Auntie's Bible, inscribed by this same queen—the woman who'd taught Lucretia to read. "But why would the king want a divorce from—"

"He be needing a heir, ninny. Catherine be giving him only a useless girl." She raised her fist in the air. "Long live the king!"

When the crowd quieted, the soldiers removed Fisher's cloak and then his shirt. Stripped of his clothing, the elderly man appeared so gaunt and feeble, a gasp rose up from the assembly. Fisher knelt and laid his bare neck on the block of wood.

A sickening nausea swirled in Dell's gut. "All these people," she stammered. "They've come to *watch*?"

"All the way from Windsor, some of them," the girl said proudly. She looked at Dell's quivering jaw. "You do be the odd duck."

"Traitor!" Someone in the crowd shouted.

"Traitor! Traitor!" other voices echoed. Sunlight reflected off the silver blade of the axe. Dell gasped for air.

These cannibals killed each other and came, with hungry eyes, to watch the killing. If the Brown Boy were here, he would take her by the hand and lead her away to a place of safety and peace.

She wriggled her hand into her pocket, withdrew the lemon and held it to her face. The man in red raised the axe over his head and brought it down with a tremendous *crack*. Dell squeezed the lemon so hard it burst open, squirting its juice into her eyes. The frenzied mob roared and raised their fists.

The executioner picked up the fallen head and held it high for all to see. "Behold the head of a traitor!"

A deafening cheer went up from the crowd. Dell rubbed her eyes. The roar was louder than a hundred rushing streams, and she was drowning, drowning. Something tugged at her sleeve.

"Come on, then," urged the girl. "They be taking it to London Bridge, to set on a pike."

"I cannot," said Dell. But the mob surged toward the bridge and swept Dell along.

The girl hung on to Dell's sleeve. "I be Margery," she shouted. "The fishmonger's daughter. On New Fish Street. Who be you?"

"Me?" Dell's mind went empty. Who *was* she? "I don't know ... that is ... Dell."

"Dell? Just *Dell*?" She twisted Dell's sleeve. "I give you three things about Margery, and *you* give only one thing. Fie on you!" She shoved Dell, and Dell felt herself sucked into the maelstrom of strangers. Margery's cap bobbed away on the wild current.

"No!" Dell cried out. "Wait!"

Margery elbowed her way back to Dell.

"I—I am a puppet master," Dell said.

Margery grabbed hold of Dell's sleeve again. "That be more like it."

A puppet master? Well, Dell *had* made two puppets. She had spent hours sewing the colorful little squares of fabric together to make Bartholomew's harlequin suit. And she *did* make him sing and tell stories. Why, even now, Bartholomew lay—albeit begrudgingly—in the bottom of her pocket. But she had no stage, no curtain, no puppet plays. Oh, how God would punish her for *this* lie. Far ahead, above the crowd, the traitor's bloody head listed back and forth on the pike.

"Please," said Dell. "I cannot continue. I am sick."

"That makes three things!" Margery crowed. "You

be Dell. You be a puppet master. And you be sick." She grabbed Dell's arm and dragged her out of the churning river of people.

Just in time. Dell turned her head and vomited.

CHAPTER
VII

Dell bent over, put both hands over her mouth, and gagged again. Bile dribbled down her chin.

Margery stood by, her foot tapping, her body smelling of dead fish. "I hope you be done soon," she said. "Because my mother be cuffing me if I don't be getting to the apothecary in time." She gave Dell a hearty whack on the back. "My brother—the puny one—Mother's precious—gots the catarrh again. The apothecary—he be bolting his door at the two o'clock bells and snoring like a mule until supper."

Dell wiped her lips. Was Margery inviting Dell to accompany her?

Margery linked her arm in Dell's. "Mark me," Margery said. "He be selling us posies also. To ward off the pestilence."

"But who would buy posies?" she said. "Violets and cowslips and wild thyme—they grow everywhere. Especially now, in the springtime."

"Do that be so?" Margery put her hands on her full hips. "You must be a cottager then, from the countryside."

Dell hesitated. A cottager. A person who lived in a cottage. Like Auntie. No, Dell was not a cottager. She lived—used to live—did not live anymore—in a cave on the mountain. Maybe she was like the crippled beggar woman after all—a girl with no means. But that wasn't true. She still had Bartholomew. And the lemon.

Margery squeezed Dell's arm so hard it hurt. "Tell me true now. In the countryside—do you be painting your face and selling your body for sweetmeats and nosegays?"

What a strange question. How could you sell your own body? And the only faces Dell had ever painted were the faces of her puppets, Bartholomew and Eleanor.

"Look out below!" A voice shouted from above. Margery grabbed Dell and yanked her into an open doorway. Something plummeted through the air and splatted nearby, just missing Dell's feet.

Margery gave a dramatic curtsy. "Why, bless you, Mistress Margery," she said airily. "You be doing Dell a fine good deed. You be saving Dell from last night's chamber pot, you do."

Dell twisted her neck and stared, open mouthed, up at the window, then back down at the brown mush at her feet.

Margery leaned close to Dell's face—oh, that smell!—and with her thumb and forefinger pinched the corners of Dell's lips together. "These you must be saving for your sweetheart. A good thing you do not be a whore."

Dell pushed Margery's hand away. Dell *had* had impure thoughts about the Boy, no doubt about it. They were like itches that she couldn't scratch. Did unclean thoughts make her a whore? She certainly wasn't anyone's sweetheart, though she wished she was. "Do whores go to the block then?" she asked. "Like traitors?"

"No, ninny. To the stocks."

An unfamiliar sound boomed through the sky like thunder. "Hang it!" Margery cried. "The bells of St. Paul's. It be two o'clock." She dragged Dell along the street and through a barely open door. The sign swinging over it said APOTHECARY. A trickle of light filtered in behind them.

When her eyes had adjusted to the dimness inside, Dell saw a shrunken old man stooped over a workbench. The bench was strewn with papers and cluttered with glass and metal objects. The man was pouring something into a small vessel. His scaly hands trembled and the liquid spilled onto his bench.

"What ails your brother today?" he said. "Ague? Apoplexy?" His nose was a sharp beak, and his white hair puffed out like feathers around his head.

"Catarrh," said Margery.

He put his hand to his ear and leaned toward Margery. "Speak up, girlie," he croaked.

"My brother gots the pickled herring," she shouted back. Then she turned to Dell and added, "He be deaf as a turd, but Mother be wanting nobody except him."

"For catarrh," said Dell. "You need nettles. Nettles and comfrey. My auntie—she knows remedies."

Margery raised one eyebrow. "Mother has comfrey at home."

"Ah," the apothecary said. "I have just the tonic." He

held up a dusty vial. "It will cure what ails your brother and ward off the pestilence as well."

"No tonic today," Margery said. She marched around the bench, cupped her hands around her mouth, and shouted into the apothecary's ear. "My mother be needing nettles. Have you any nettles?"

"Nipples?"

"Nettles!" she shouted even louder. "If you cannot be selling them to me, I be going to the midwife."

"Bah," he muttered and removed a bottle from the shelf. He tore a small square off the corner of one of the big papers on his bench. Dell stepped closer. The whole paper was covered with words. The apothecary shook the nettles from the bottle onto the square of paper, then folded the paper into a neat package.

Dell hung behind Margery. She squinted, straining to see the words, but too afraid of the old man to step close. At home, the words in Auntie's Bible had always helped Dell to understand things. "What is it?" she asked.

"What do you think, ninny?" Margery said, waving the package. "Nettles."

"No." Dell pointed at the long sheet of paper, torn, but still full of words. "That."

The old man snatched the paper from the bench. He ripped off another strip and shook it at Dell. "I don't give a fig what this handbill says. I'll bow to neither king *nor* Pope."

Margery brought a finger to her lips. "Quiet, you old fool."

"I shan't bow to anyone because I *cannot*." He cackled. "My legs are too brittle." He stuffed the strip of paper—words and all—into his mouth and chewed furiously. The wad of paper bulged as it went down his throat.

Margery lined up three coins on the bench.

The apothecary crushed the rest of the handbill into a wad and pushed it at them. "Arse-wisp is what this is good for." He turned and wagged his shrunken backside at them to make his point.

Margery dropped the ball of crushed paper into her pocket. "A good use it be then," she said, "for my brother gots the squitters, too." She reached for Dell's hand, and Dell stumbled out the door behind her.

"Posies," he shouted after them. "Tied and ready to hang about your neck."

Dell blinked in the bright sunlight, a relief after the frightening and dusty tomb of the shop. They walked until they came to an ale house with a bench in front.

"Shall we read it, then?" Dell asked.

"Read it?" Margery stopped and set her hands on her hips. "Read it?" she said again. "What do you fancy yourself? A schoolboy? A priest? A fine lady? Oh, by all means, read to Margery from the arse-wisp." She settled herself on the ale house bench, took the handbill from her pocket, and pressed it out flat. She motioned Dell to sit.

"Tush," Margery said. "I can read as well as the likes of you." She put her finger on a large letter *E* that began the word *England*. "See. Here be a *F*. Like in *fishmonger*."

Margery crossed her arms and drew herself up as straight as the blackened timber behind her.

Dell's mouth hung open. Margery, the girl who stank of dead fish and knew everything, did not know how to read. "Can you not—"

"My mother," Margery said, "be teaching me how to keep fleas from the bed, how to pickle eel, and how to salt pike."

"Have you no book?"

"We gots a ledger book." She ran her finger over the crumpled paper until she came to the number VIII. "Here be a eight," she said. "Every shilling, I keep count in my da's book."

Dell leaned over the crumpled handbill and read the words that had not been torn off or swallowed by the apothecary.

Margery's fishy smell and her ample body hovered over the paper. "Speak up," she said.

Dell inched away from Margery. If she came too close to Dell's pocket, she would feel the lump that was Bartholomew and demand to see him. Dell pulled her skirt close. "These words," she said. "I can read them, but I can make no sense of them."

"What is the use of reading then?" Margery said. "We would do better to listen to the bleating of a nanny goat."

Dell read anyway. "The king, not the Pope, is the supreme head of the Church of England." The king head of the church? This writing was all backward. The king wasn't the head of the church. The Pope was. Even *she* knew that. "Any seditious writing or talk—"

"Seditious." Dell glanced at Margery. "Do you know the meaning of that word?" But Margery only spread her legs apart and fanned the inside of her thighs with her skirt.

A shadow fell across Dell's shoulders and she looked up, startled. Behind her stood a tall man with strawlike hair. Dell pulled the handbill close to her breast.

The man crossed his arms over his big apron. "Well mark that. A rustic who knows how to read."

Heat rose in Dell's cheeks. How could the man tell that she was not from the city? Maybe if she had a cap with ribbons, like all the other women, she would look as if she belonged.

Margery tipped up her chin. "I be clever also. But that be no concern of yours."

The man continued to look at Dell. "Seditious," he mused, as if he were talking to himself. "Words that rile up the people against the king."

Dell's curiosity overcame her fear of the stranger. "But who would go against the king? Why?"

"Indeed," said the man. He removed his cap and drew his fingers through his haystack hair. "If you are in need of work, I am in need of someone to read to my blind father."

Dell inched closer to Margery.

"Ha!" Margery snapped her legs together and narrowed her eyes at the stranger. "Methinks you be looking for a simple girl to take for a amble." She grabbed Dell's arm. "Well, this one be with me."

"I see," the man said. He tipped his flat cap at Dell. "I'm John the Joiner. On Carpenter Lane. Good day." He continued along the street, whistling a merry tune.

Dell let out her breath—thank Heaven Margery had defended her from the strange man. Dell continued reading where she had left off. *"Any seditious writing or talk shall be considered treason against the crown."* She shuddered. That word again. *Treason.*

Margery shrugged. "Arse-wisp." She snatched up the handbill and stuffed it back in her pocket. "It be late. We needs be getting home."

Home. Well, Dell didn't have a home. And in this city she was no one. But she did have Bartholomew and the lemon. And a girl at her side. Still, an aching feeling curled around Dell's heart. If only she could find the Boy.

CHAPTER

VIII

Dell struggled to keep pace with Margery, whose solid body gave Dell a sense of safety and comfort. She tried to keep her eyes down on the muddy street and up on the bustling people at the same time, so she wouldn't slip in the muck or miss the Boy, should he happen to walk by. If only she knew his name. If only he knew hers.

While they hurried along, she listened to Margery's constant prattle, trying to glean every kernel of information she could. The effort made her dizzy. They rushed on, along streets so narrow and past buildings so tall and close, it seemed as if day had turned to eventide. The buildings looked strange and yet familiar, as if she'd walked these streets before.

They had just left Pie Corner when a loud crash interrupted Margery's chatter. Sounds of splintering and cracking overpowered the din of the street. Up ahead, soldiers milled outside a church, wielding axes and halberds. Dell stopped in her tracks. Had they found a traitor inside the church? Would they kill him?

Margery nudged her forward. "Pay them no heed," she said. "They only be carrying out the king's command."

One soldier was balanced high on a ladder, before a

window of colored glass. The pieces of glass formed a picture—Eve holding out the apple to Adam. And beside them the fork-tongued serpent. The soldier drew back his axe and smashed it into the window. Shards of every color fell to the earth. Dell gasped.

Another soldier marched out of the church, his arms piled with objects—a plate, a chalice, a censer, and a large crucifix—all made of silver and gold. He tossed his load into a cart as carelessly as Father threw logs onto the woodpile.

"They're plundering the church," Dell whispered. More sounds of chopping and cracking. "Can no one stop them?"

"Who would stop the king's soldiers? They be obeying the king. The churches be his now."

Another crash made Dell jump. "But a church is the house of God. Even a king has no right—"

Margery grabbed Dell's ear and jerked it close to her lips. "Didn't you see what happens to those who question the king?" she whispered. Dell recoiled from Margery's fishy breath but stayed close at her side.

Dell smelled the river's fishiness and felt its clammy wetness even before she saw its sulky waters. Margery walked faster now, and the immense body of water came into view. A myriad of slim boats glided along its murky darkness, and a great bridge crossed it. The bridge was lined—from one end to the other—with tall buildings. Dell gawked at its strangeness. It didn't seem possible—dozens and dozens of buildings on a bridge. How different it was from the wobbly log that carried her across the stream.

"There," Margery said, pointing at the bridge. "There be the heads of traitors, on pikes."

"That can't be," Dell choked. From this distance they looked like a great display of puppet heads.

Margery marched forward. "Long live the king!"

"Long live the king," Dell mumbled and hurried to keep pace with Margery.

The ground beneath her feet grew spongy and soft, and its wetness soaked through her thin leather shoes. Her feet, which were already damp from the mud, became thoroughly soaked. She squelched along, trying not to think about the display of heads.

"When Margery be the wife of a rich man," Margery said, "she shan't be sogging her feet with walking. She be hiring a wherry to travel up and down the river. Though to tell you true, I may rather be traveling by horse or by carriage, for I do be afeared of drowning."

Dell nodded distractedly. The river was so wide, so different from the stream on the mountain. The stream had banks—edges. It knew exactly where water ended and land began. But the river, it seemed, observed no such boundaries. It simply sloshed ever outward into a sodden and reedy marsh. Bartholomew, with his clear convictions about being a performer, was like the stream—surging ever forward. She felt like the river, sloshing about, murky and unsure.

"And you must not cross the bridge," Margery went on. "All manner of sinners lurk there. Cutpurses and actors and bear-baiters and whores."

Maybe that was why Dell hadn't seen any cannibals in this part of the city—they all lived across the river. Well, at least she wouldn't have to look for the Brown Boy there. "What about traitors?" she asked. "Do they lurk there?"

"No, ninny. Traitors be locked in the Tower until they be executed."

At last they arrived at a building that looked exactly like scores of other buildings Dell had seen that day. It had the same walls, supported by black timbers and gray with soil. Next to the door was a window and above that window, another window. And above the higher-up window sloped a roof made of smooth flat tiles. And from the roof rose a chimney, and from the chimney, smoke.

"Home," Margery announced. A sign hanging out over the door said FISHMONGER, and below the word was a picture of a fish. The fish had small round eyes and a wide open mouth.

Dell stared at the sign, hoping she did not look as dull and stupid as the fish, and then she returned her gaze to the chimney. The smoke meant that a fire burned somewhere inside the house. Dell prayed that the unseen fire did not roast human flesh.

Outside the door a large man leaned over a stump,

cleaning a fish. Four small children squatted on the ground near his feet. They were stacking tiny fish bones into a tower. When the smallest child, a boy even shorter than Nathaniel, caught sight of Margery, he leapt up, squealed in delight, then rammed his head into her leg.

"Oh, Luke," she moaned in mock agony, "you gots me sorely." She pointed at the children one at a time. "Matthew, Mark, Luke, and Jennet," she said. Then she nodded at the man. "And that be my da."

Margery's father raised his knife and with a quick flick of his wrist, cut off the fish's head. "What idleness led you astray today?" he said, slicing into the fish. "Ned coughs near to die."

Margery crossed her arms over her chest. "Ned always coughs near to die," she retorted in a sullen voice.

Dell sucked in her breath. Certainly Margery's father would not tolerate such insolent talk. But he simply picked up the fish head and tossed it into a pail next to the stump.

"Coughing Ned, I calls my brother." She led Dell through the open door into a room with a fire burning in it. The room smelled even fishier than Margery, but when Dell edged close to the hearth—praise God!—no human flesh bubbled in the cauldron.

Margery took the package of comfrey off the shelf and set it on the table beside the nettles. Then she brought in a pot of grayish water for washing and hung another pot of ale over the fire to boil.

After Dell scrubbed her hands, she crushed the herbs

with a mortar and pestle and added them to the ale. When the mixture was steamy and aromatic, Dell took a sip. Yes, it tasted like Auntie's. Or close enough.

Margery poured it into a cup and motioned Dell to follow her up a series of steps that rose on their right. Although Dell had often climbed rocky embankments on the mountain, she'd never climbed steps before, and she ascended slowly.

At the top was another room that contained three straw mattresses. On one mattress lay a boy so frail he barely formed a lump beneath the sheet. His face was rosy with fever, his eyes sunken.

A woman knelt beside him. With one hand she held a shawl around her shoulders, and with the other she pressed a damp rag on the boy's forehead. The boy coughed a cough so gritty and thick with phlegm, it seemed it would crack his ribcage in two.

The floorboard creaked beneath Margery's feet. "He *do* be bad," she whispered. "He be very bad indeed." She set the cup beside her mother and backed away.

"Go," said the woman without turning to look at Margery. "Tend to the little ones." Ned coughed again, and his body rattled as if riddled by demons.

Margery grabbed Dell's hand and dragged her, tripping and stumbling, down the steps.

CHAPTER
IX

A squeal came from outside. Margery's little sister, Jennet, galloped into the room, waving her arms and screaming at Luke, who clung to her tangled hair. The two of them crashed into Dell, and she stumbled backward.

Margery grabbed up the broom and swatted Luke on his backside. "For shame!" she cried. "Your own Ned be near to die, and you frolic like kittens." She raised the broom over her head. "Off with you!"

Ned coughed again, and Dell could feel the pain inside her own chest—and then a flash—a memory of herself coughing—and then a thick caudle spooned between her lips, the taste of honey and lemon, a gentle hand cradling her head. She must be remembering her mother—no one else in her family had a tender touch.

Honey and lemon. They might calm Ned's cough the way they had once calmed hers. But the lemon belonged to Dell and—torn or whole— she needed it. The feel of it in her pocket comforted her, made her feel—what? Less alone?

Jennet poked her head around the doorway. "Ned die?" she asked.

"Have you any honey?" Dell blurted out, and instantly wished she hadn't.

"Honey? Look about you. Do we be drinking from goblets of glass? Do we be dressing in taffeta? This be the house of a fishmonger." Margery narrowed her eyes at Dell. "Why do you needs honey?"

Dell squeezed the lemon so tightly that juice dribbled over her fingers. "It will quiet Ned's cough."

Margery raised her eyebrows.

"It's a remedy my mother gave to me. A long time ago."

Margery jingled the remaining coins in her purse. "Honey Lane aren't far. Do you needs much?"

"A spoonful," Dell said. "Two or three if you can pay."

"I be quick as a arrow." Margery retied the ribbons more tightly on her cap, grabbed a wooden cup off the table, and bolted out the door.

"Wait," Dell called after her. "You must buy a lemon also." She ran to the doorway and looked out. The street was teeming with people and animals, but Margery was nowhere in sight.

Had Dell told Margery the truth about the honey and lemon? Dell licked at her fingers. Yes, she felt certain that the memory was real—that she had sipped honey and lemon from her mother's spoon.

But the memory was fading now, and Dell felt hollow inside, dry. Probably from thirst. Her lips were cracked, her tongue gritty. The last time she'd eaten or taken a sip of water was that morning, at the stream. A lifetime ago, it seemed.

The clang of bells rattled the sky again. Two, three, four peals rang out. The day was rolling, fast as a tumbling weed, into evening. She needed to find the Brown Boy, but she would never be able to find him in the dark. Dell shivered. If the City of Cannibals was frightening and confusing in the day, what would it be like at night?

She leaned out the doorway and peered up and down the street. The agitated sound of Ned's coughing sawed like a dull knife on her flesh, and she paced back and forth, door to hearth, hearth to door.

She took the lemon out of her pocket. She certainly wasn't going use *her* lemon on Ned. He wasn't *her* brother, after all. *Her* brother was Nathaniel, and despite his surliness of late, she would gladly give up her lemon for him. But this Ned—he was nothing but a stranger. When Margery came back, Dell would have to send her out a second time to buy a lemon. She had just turned from the doorway when Margery burst into the room, panting.

"I gots the honey. Three spoonfuls I got."

Dell straightened her back. "You need to get one more thing."

"One more thing?" Margery said. She yanked off her cap and her russet curls sprang out. "Well, I aren't getting one more thing because I spent every farthing on the honey."

Dell shrank back. The nubby fruit lay like a millstone in her pocket. "The honey is of no use without a lemon."

"A what?" Margery demanded. Her rank smell suffocated Dell, and the heat of the fire scorched her back.

"A lemon," Dell repeated. "If we mix the juice of a lemon with the honey, it will soothe Ned's cough."

"I think you be mad." Margery reached for the broom. "Or else a witch." She raised the broom over her head.

"I'm not ... I ..." Dell yanked the lemon from her pocket and held it out. She stared at the lemon as if it were her own heart lying in her outstretched hand.

Margery lowered the broom and craned her neck toward the lemon. "The food of the devil is what that be, for I never be seeing such a thing in my life."

"They grow here," Dell choked out. "I know they do. The Brown Boy—"

"Of course they don't grows here, ninny."

Margery took the lemon and turned it round and round in her hand. "What be the taste?"

"See for yourself."

Margery wriggled her finger in the torn place of the lemon, then brought her finger to her tongue. "Oh," she said. She pursed her lips. "A surprise! A sour surprise!"

Dell wished for some surprises, too. She wished another lemon would magically appear so she would not have to use hers. She wished the Brown Boy would appear, too, and scoop her up in his arms and carry her away.

But she also wished for Ned to stop coughing, so he could sleep through the night and get better. It was up to her. If she gave up her lemon, Ned at least had a chance.

Dell picked up a knife, then set the lemon on the trestle

table and cut it slowly in two. She squeezed every drop of juice into the cup, picked out the seeds that had fallen in, and stirred the juice into the honey.

Margery licked at the pulpy remains and shivered. "This be a *nice* sour, better than the sour of bad ale."

"We can take it up now."

"You go on," Margery said. "I needs be warming the sauce for supper."

"Go up? Alone?"

"You be wanting Ned to live and the rest of us starve? Do you not be hungry?"

Of course Dell was hungry. Hungry and thirsty. She'd had nothing to drink since that tiny sip from the cauldron. Her legs wobbled and her tongue felt thick. Bartholomew was lucky. He never had to worry about food or drink or *anything*. Dell always made sure he was safe. But was he grateful to her? Was he content? Oh, no. He wanted to parade himself in front of the whole world. She wished *she* was small and hidden and safe, like him.

One by one, she climbed the narrow, creaky stairs.

CHAPTER

X

As Dell entered the upstairs room, the floorboards groaned beneath her feet.

"Margery? Be that you?"

"No," Dell said. "I'm a friend ... an acquaintance of Margery's. I've brought something to quiet Ned's cough. So he can keep his medicine down." She held out the cup.

Ned's breath was ragged, and his hair, which was the same orange as Margery's, lay in sweaty clumps around his head.

Margery's mother pulled her shawl close and hunched her shoulders. "Do you know how many babes I be burying already? Three. Three innocent babes."

Ned retched again, and Margery's mother took the cup from Dell. She dipped her finger in the mixture, tasted it, and puckered her lips. With a sigh, she leaned over her son and spooned a few drops between his lips. Her shawl fell to the floor, but she seemed not to notice, and Dell thought it best to keep out of the way.

After awhile the stairs creaked, and Margery appeared in the doorway. In her hand she carried a trencher and under her arm a loaf of barley bread. "Da and the little ones be fed," she said to her mother, who did not look up.

"I come with your supper." She set the trencher and bread next to her mother's stool. "Your supper, Mother."

A moment later the four younger children straggled upstairs. After they said their prayers, they piled into the larger bed. Matthew and Mark laid their heads at one end, and Luke and Jennet laid theirs at the other.

"Mother," Margery repeated. "Your supper."

Heavier footsteps clumped up the steps. Margery's father entered the room with a candle, and its flickering light made his shadow leap, like an angry hobgoblin, on the wall. Dell shrank back. What if ordinary men became cannibals at night?

She waited to see if he might roar or lick his chops. But he simply picked up his wife's shawl and laid it over her shoulders. Then he set the candle down beside her and with a sigh, lay down on the remaining bed.

Margery turned to Dell. "Your supper be on the table in the kitchen. Go down to it quickly or the rats be feasting."

Dell crept down the stairs. On the table sat a still-steaming trencher. Chunks of something pale poked out of the thick sauce. She leaned close and sniffed. It smelled like fish. Her mouth watered. If those were pieces of human flesh—well, God forgive her. She soaked a chunk of bread in the rich sauce and nibbled at its edge. Nothing in her life had ever tasted so delicious.

She stuffed another piece—still dripping—into her mouth. She had barely swallowed it when she shoveled in another chunk of bread and then another. She ate like a glutton, not stopping until she had wiped the trencher clean.

She lay down on the narrow bench, on her left side, so as not to crush Bartholomew. She longed to go back upstairs and curl up in the cozy nest of Margery's family. But she couldn't. She didn't belong. At least she had Bartholomew. And until she found the Boy, her puppet would have to suffice.

"Wake up, lazy," a voice commanded. Someone pinched Dell's rump, and she tumbled off the bench onto the reed-covered floor. Where was she? She sat up and rubbed her eyes. Above her stood Margery, a steaming bowl in hand.

"Ned," Dell murmured, looking all around. "What about Ned?"

Margery set the bowl on the table beside Dell. "Come and see."

As they climbed the stairs, the three older boys came crashing past them. The biggest, Matthew, was pounding Mark's head with his fist. "Mark be pissing the bed again!"

Mark swung out with his arms. "Did not!" he screamed. "It be Luke. Luke be pissing it."

Dell dodged their flailing arms and scrambled into the tiny room. Sure enough—there lay Ned, eyes half-open, head propped on a pillow.

A smile flitted across Dell's face. The honey and lemon

had really worked! Even though it had grieved her to part with the lemon, at least her sacrifice had mattered.

Margery set her hands on her hips. "Look lively, now," she commanded her brother. "This be the girl."

Dell's cheeks grew warm with embarrassment. "I didn't do it alone." She reached into her pocket and an instant later was joggling Bartholomew in front of Ned. "I also had help from my friend here."

The boy's eyes opened wider.

Bartholomew bowed. Then he bobbed right up to Ned and squeezed the child's nose, *honk, honk.*

When Ned gave a faint smile, Bartholomew became inspired. He mewed like a pussy cat, quacked like a duck, and broke into a chorus of *hey, nonny, nonny no.*

Margery stared open-mouthed at Dell. "Why, you *do* be a puppeteer. But who be teaching you the craft?"

"My mother was a puppeteer," she said. And then to herself—*my mother was a puppeteer.* How good it felt to know something true about her past. *And I am a puppeteer as well.*

"Margery," their father's voice boomed outside. "Make haste."

Margery dragged Dell down the steps. "Now we be even," she said. "I be saving you from the chamber pot, and you be saving Ned from an early grave." They hurried past the bowl of pottage on the table and out the door.

"It be light already," said Margery's father, "and here you be standing idle."

Margery hurried to a large trough full of water. At the bottom floated small white objects Dell had never seen before. Margery picked them out and arranged them in a basket.

"How do you expect to be a fit wife," continued her father, "if you needs be prodded like a mule."

Margery puffed herself up. "I shan't marry the tanner, if that be your meaning. He be scratching his ass all day long, and pus be dripping out his ear."

"Who then? Not King Henry, I daresay, for he gots himself a second wife and don't be needing a third." A playful smile flickered at the corners of his lips. "Especially not the likes of you."

Margery lowered her voice. "That aren't what they be saying at the market. The gossip be that the king *do* want a third wife. One that can bear him a son."

"Watch your tongue, girl. Men have gone to the scaffold for such talk. Go peddle the oysters while they be fresh."

Dell hung back. She needed to find the Brown Boy, but the city was so frightening and confusing.

Margery marched off, then stopped and glanced over her shoulder at Dell. "Do you be coming or no? I aren't got all day."

Dell ran to her side, then struggled to keep up as Margery scurried along the winding streets and narrow alleys.

After awhile Margery slowed her pace. "This be Cheapside. A good place for selling." She held her basket out in front of her, just below her ample bosoms. "Fresh oysters!" she shouted. "The finest oysters for your table!"

They passed stall after stall after stall—everything in the world, it seemed, could be bought or sold—and a whole row of goldsmith shops, then fullers and spurriers, saddlers and dyers, and beside a tavern, a woman washing linens in a tub over a fire. Dell's eyes followed the curl of rising smoke and wondered if Father or Auntie or Nathaniel could see it, too. *You know what burns in those fires. You know.* But the truth was, Dell *didn't* know—she hadn't seen a single cannibal so far—and she needed to settle the matter once and for all.

She grabbed Margery's sleeve. "Tell me," she said in a choking voice. "Are there cannibals in the city?"

"Cannibals?" Margery cried. "The kind that eats people?"

Dell nodded, barely able to breathe.

"No, ninny. But I hear they be living up in the hills outside the city walls."

"Oh, no," Dell gasped. "I am certain they do not. Who told you such a story?"

Margery shrugged. "My da. But to tell you true—I think he just be trying to scare us so we don't be running off."

Dell tripped over a stone. So that was it. Father had done the same thing—he had told her lies about cannibals so she would be afraid to come to the city. And she had believed him.

They hurried on until they came to a large square. It was empty of buildings but swarming with people and animals. Beside it rose the biggest, most magnificent building Dell had ever seen. She stood there, gawking at its towering stone walls and its windows of colored glass.

"It just be a church," said Margery. "St. Paul's." Her gaze rose up to the tip of the towering steeple. "Though I suppose it do be a great church."

"And have the soldiers plundered this one also?"

Margery gave her a sharp jab in the ribs. "The king's soldiers don't be *plundering*. They be *removing* things. For the king. But—good Heaven, no—not St. Paul's."

The instant she stepped onto the square, Dell was pushed and jostled and squeezed. While Margery haggled with a woman over the price of a dozen oysters, Dell noticed a boy who was juggling four balls—a red, a blue, a yellow, and a green. If only her brother could see this! Nathaniel had tried to juggle four pinecones at once, but he could only keep three going.

Dell's gaze moved downward, from the spinning balls to the boy poised beneath them. Like Nathaniel, the juggler was short of stature. He wore saggy green tights, a red tunic, and a hat with little silver bells that jingled when he leaned sideways to catch the balls.

His legs, his arms, his torso were just like Nathaniel's. He had the same thick eyebrows on his cliff of a brow. But he also had a thick black beard. The juggler wasn't a boy at all. He was a grown man.

Dell stood, gawking at him.

"Surely you gots jugglers in the countryside?" Margery nudged Dell with the edge of her basket. "If you don't shuts your mouth, somebody be snaggling a hook in it." She tapped her foot impatiently. "He aren't a cannibal, if that be your thinking."

"He looks like ... like ..."

"Like a juggling dwarf, ninny."

"A dwarf," Dell said, trying out the word to see how it felt on her lips. The word caught in her mouth like a real fish hook, twisting and pulling until she choked for air. A dwarf. So that's what Father was. And Auntie and Nathaniel, too—dwarfs. She looked around at the ocean of people who were as tall or taller than she. "Are there many other dwarfs in the city?"

Margery crooked her arm in Dell's and marched her past the juggler. "I aren't the census-keeper now, are I? I count my da's money and his oysters and that be all I count. But if you needs know, I suppose the dwarfs be some and not so many."

Dell leaned into Margery, grateful for her sturdy arm. How could Dell have been so slow to understand? She and her mother weren't the ones who looked different. It was Father and Auntie and Nathaniel.

And yet, for some reason, Lucretia had loved Father, even though she was tall and beautiful and he was a dwarf. Auntie had said he'd helped her escape the palace. Is that why Lucretia loved him?

Dell's head throbbed. Well, even if she *looked* the same as everyone else here, she was different inside. She was still a stranger who didn't belong.

"The king keeps dwarfs at court for amusement. But they be the lucky ones. Most be paupers working in the streets."

Dell turned and stared over her shoulder. The juggler had set down his balls and was walking on his hands, the way Nathaniel used to do. Had Father walked on his hands before the king, too? And later, on the streets?

Maybe the Brown Boy, who always knew what supplies to bring to her family, also knew about her family's past. When—*if*—Dell found him, she would ask him these questions, and more. Margery continued to pull her through the crowd, and everywhere the cry was the same.

"What do you lack?" shouted a seller of vegetables.

"What do you lack?" shouted a butcher in a blood-stained apron.

"What do you lack?" shouted a girl with colorful ribbons draped all along her arms.

Margery elbowed her way across the square. Terrified of being separated from her, Dell clung to the girl's sleeve. She peered over the heads of people when she could, straining for a glimpse of the Brown Boy.

Dell saw him first, but Margery let loose the exclamation.

CHAPTER

XI

"There he be!" Margery clenched her hands to her bosom. "Oh, my heart! Aren't he the beautiful one!"

The Brown Boy stood across the street from the square. He was helping a man fit a hoop around a barrel.

Dumbstruck, Dell looked first at Margery, then at the Brown Boy, then back at Margery.

"See how he be standing tall and straight as the king's guard," Margery went on. "And his eyes, as big and brown as the eyes of a bull at slaughter. And his smile. Oh, how Margery would swoon to see him smile on her."

Dell stared at the broad back of the Brown Boy. *Her* Brown Boy. She tried to speak, but the words stuck—like crumbs of dry bread—in her throat. "Do you know him?" she finally asked, her voice small and hoarse.

"Ronaldo? Of course I knows him," Margery said. She pinched her white cheeks until they flushed rosy, then she fluffed her russet curls. "And I would be well-pleased were he to plant a kiss on these." With that, she stretched out her neck, squeezed her eyes shut, and pursed her lips.

Dell pulled her tangled hair behind her ear. "But—"

Margery opened her eyes. "But he be promised to God," she said and sighed deeply.

"Promised to God?"

Margery threw up her hands. "Do you know nothing? Have you not eyes to see his habit, the cut of his hair? He be a novice. On the Feast Day of St. James—before summer's end—he be getting ordained a Benedictine priest. And then Heaven help poor Margery!"

She grabbed Dell's clammy hand and placed it on her own bosom. Dell, choking on Margery's fishy smell, tried to pull away, but Margery held on tightly. "Feel how my poor heart beats when he is close."

Dell nodded. Her own heart was thumping so loudly, it drowned out the sound of Margery's. The Brown Boy continued at his task, deaf to the beating of their hearts.

"But," Margery went on, "today his beauty still belongs to the world. And most especially to Margery." With that, she thrust out her bosoms, propped her basket on one hip, and strode toward the Boy, her skirt swaying. A cart swerved to avoid hitting her. The driver cursed, but Margery kept her chin up and marched forward.

Dell did not follow. Even if Margery had invited her, she could not have followed. She stood, like a tree, at the edge of the square. Her arms were stiff as the branches of the yew, and her feet had taken root in the cracks between the stones. She tried to speak, but her tongue—dry as a winter leaf—filled up her mouth.

Ronaldo was pressing his weight on the lid of the barrel when Margery sidled up to him. She leaned over him so close that one of her breasts brushed his back. Ronaldo turned, and without even pinching his nose, he drew back his shoulders and smiled.

Dell didn't move. At last she had found the Brown Boy. All she had to do was cross the square and show herself to him. Tell him that *she* was the one who came to him when the moon waned to its slenderest self. It was *she* who could recognize his easy gait as he walked along the path. *She* who knew the rise and fall of his chest as he dozed, the gentle timbre of his voice.

And his smile, the smile he had just shared with Margery. Dell could recognize that smile anywhere. She could see it in the darkest dark of a moonless night. And yet she could not move. Only her heart moved, pounding like tromping feet, feet running fast and hard and far away from Margery and Ronaldo.

Margery reached into her basket and withdrew something. An oyster? Then she held it up to the boy's face. A puzzled look replaced Ronaldo's smile, and he took the object from Margery. Dell craned her neck forward. It was a piece of lemon rind.

Ronaldo tossed it from hand to hand. Margery's lips moved with her busy chatter, but Ronaldo looked right over her head, across the busy street where Dell stood, gaping at him. She ducked behind a sack of onions and held her breath.

She longed to run across the street, to claim the lemon as her own, to claim the Boy as her own, but her body remained as inert as the sack of onions.

"What is your business?" said a gruff voice on the other side of the sack. "If you be buying, buy. If you be thieving, I shall take this knife to your thumbs."

Dell struggled to her feet, unable to take her eyes off Margery and the Boy.

Margery, still chattering, took the lemon rind from the Boy and pointed at his mouth. Ronaldo pushed out his tongue. Laughing, Margery squeezed the rind over it. Dell thought she had crushed the fruit dry, but Ronaldo startled as a sour drop touched his tongue. He wiped his lips with his sleeve and laughed along with Margery. Then— carelessly—thoughtlessly—she tossed the remains of the lemon—Dell's lemon—into the gutter.

"You be slow-witted, I see," said the onion seller, shaking his head. "Well, a slow wit be punishment enough in this world. You needn't starve also." He reached into the sack and pushed an onion into Dell's hand.

As she stood gaping, a man on a great white horse clumped onto the square, and for a moment, blocked her view of the Boy. The man wore a fine cloak and an ermine-trimmed hat, and people lowered their eyes as he passed by. With each step of his horse, the man's jowls jiggled, but his back remained rigid.

Dell thought about the horse that had toppled the booth and crushed her mother to death. She'd always imagined the horse being a small, high-strung creature. Black. But maybe it had been white and powerful, like this one. The horse paused, pawing at the earth with his hairy hoofs. Ronaldo pulled up his hood and disappeared into the crowd.

"Well, move on then," said the onion seller. "I don't want a half-wit drooling on my onions."

Dell nodded, but her gaze was fixed on the wide rump of the horse as it pranced away.

"Did you hear me now?" said the man. "Off with you."

"Yes," Dell said. "Yes, I hear you." She looked down at the onion—how had it gotten into her hand?—and then she turned and ran. She pushed her way through the throng of people. Tears filled her eyes and the square blurred. Roosters crowed, chickens squawked, a bull bellowed. The bells of St. Paul's—so close and so loud now—rang out and shook the sky. Everywhere voices shouted, *What do you lack? What do you need?*

Dell clapped her hands over her ears. What *didn't* she lack? She lacked a home where she belonged. She lacked knowledge about her own past. She lacked hope that the Boy could ever be hers. And now she didn't even have her lemon.

Her foot hit something hard and she sent a pyramid of apples tumbling. Behind her a robust voice shouted, "Indulgences! Indulgences for the forgiveness of sins." She ran faster, weaving around carts and baskets and barrels.

She collapsed in a stinking alley and drew her legs close to stop their trembling. She pushed her hands into her pockets. One was empty, save for a damp lemon seed. But in the other lay Bartholomew, secure and in one piece.

The lemon had led her to the Boy, just as she'd hoped.

She'd found him, but in the same instant, lost him to God. Or maybe to Margery, she wasn't sure

A few people hurried past, but no one cast a downward glance. To the passersby, she was just a nameless beggar who mattered to no one. She pressed her back against the wall, attentive, watchful.

The alley grew dark and chilly, and the clatter of the day quieted. The bells pealed vespers. Dell's smock was still moist with the sweat of running, and she shivered. Just past a pile of slops, the remains of a tiny fire smoldered.

She removed Bartholomew from her pocket and held him to her breast.

"Oh, Bartholomew," she said. "What have I done?"

"Done?" He pushed himself from her embrace. "Why, you have run away from the Brown Boy and from Margery. And now you are feeling sorry for yourself because you are all alone. Unless you count the rats as company, in which case you have a great congregation of friends."

Dell grasped Bartholomew's chin in her hand. "Why do you never understand? I'm not like Margery. I don't know how to tease a boy the way she does. Or touch one."

"Margery seemed to want you for a friend."

"She doesn't know me. Soon enough she would see me for who I truly am."

"Would that someone would see *me* for who *I* am,"

Bartholomew said, giving Dell a peeved look. "But how can they, as long as I'm a prisoner in your pocket?"

"I'm keeping you safe," she said.

"Thank you," he said indignantly. "But I never asked for safety." He shivered. "The day grows cold. You would do well to build up the fire."

She stuffed him in her pocket and pushed herself to her feet. She found a broken spoke from a wheel, a filthy rag, and a few shaggy roots encrusted on a shattered pot. They were poor kindling, but maybe sufficient for a small fire—enough to warm her fingers. Or the onion.

Along the wall crept a rat. If the rats were out, evening was close at hand. And after evening would come night. She stared into the smoke and Ronaldo's face began to take shape. Even if he were promised to God, he could still talk to her, couldn't he?

She laid her onion in the ashes and turned it over and over until its outer skin grew warm. The first layer was gritty with ash, but the inner layers were sweet and crunchy and surprisingly good. After she had eaten every morsel and licked the juice off her fingers, she struggled to stay alert. A hungry rat would eat anything.

CHAPTER

XII

"Look out below!" a voice shouted. Still half asleep, Dell flew to her feet. The contents of a chamber pot splattered her shoes but missed her dress. Thank Heaven Margery had taught her the meaning of that call.

The alley was tinged with light now, and she looked down at her once-blue skirt. It was gray now—dirty gray— like the sky. At the tip of her shoe was a ragged hole that hadn't been there last night. The work of a rat. She wriggled her finger inside the hole to her damp stocking. At least the rat hadn't nibbled through her pocket to Bartholomew.

People bustled along the alley, laughing and calling to one another. They were—all of them—brothers or sisters, cousins or friends, neighbors or work fellows. Every one of them was a part of some great and mysterious mosaic. Everyone except her. How could she be in the midst of so many people and feel so alone?

She felt angry, suddenly, at Ronaldo. Why hadn't he seen her yesterday? He'd been close enough—barely a stone's throw away. But how could he have seen her? She'd acted the coward, hiding behind a sack of onions and then running away. Well, she wouldn't do *that* again.

She passed unfamiliar shops and stalls and churches

she'd never seen before. From a tavern came angry shouts. The sign swinging above the open door said THE KING'S HEAD. "Out!" a woman's voice shouted. "Out, I say!"

A girl about Dell's age stumbled headfirst out the door. She stopped and spun around. "You cheated me," she yelled. "I will tell the whole city, I will. Blanche of The King's Head cheated me." She turned and stomped past Dell.

A red-faced woman thrust her head out the door. "Thief!" she shouted.

"Liar!" yelled the girl.

The woman marched after the girl, waving a pewter spoon in the air. "Gallows take you!"

The red-faced woman stopped and turned on Dell. "You see what I found in her bosom!" she shouted, shaking the spoon in Dell's face. "A thief she is. And what is worse— now I have no help!"

Dell backed away, but the woman pursued her.

"Are you deaf and dumb, wench? What think you of *that*?"

"I think God will punish her for her sin," Dell whispered.

"Of course God will punish her," the woman shouted. "But what of *me*?" She poked Dell with the spoon. "Did you not hear me? I—have—no—help."

"I could help you," Dell said. If she didn't find work, she would have to beg, like the woman with no legs. And besides, work would make her useful, a part of something.

The woman grabbed Dell's ear and dragged her inside

the tavern. "Do you steal?" she demanded, twisting Dell's ear.

"Ow," Dell whimpered, trying to pull away. "I am no thief."

"Are you lazy?"

"Sometimes."

The woman twisted her ear even tighter.

"Please, mistress, you're hurting me. No, please, I am not lazy."

The woman let go and thrust a rag in Dell's hand. "Scrub the tables. And when you are done, add fresh rushes to the old ones on the floor. And rinse the plates and tankards. And if I find a pewter spoon slipped between your bosoms, I will send you to the gallows. Do you hear me?"

"Yes, mistress," Dell said. "And if it please you, might I have something to eat and drink?"

"Eat? What have you done to earn your bread, you lazy wench?"

"Nothing," Dell said. "But—"

"Then get to work." The woman whirled around, then spun back. "Your name, wench."

"Dell."

"Your proper name."

"Dell," Dell repeated. "It is the only name I have."

"Ah, I see how it is," the woman said. One side of her mouth quivered into a crooked smile. "Your mother was too poor to give you a proper name."

Dell twisted the rag in her hands.

"That was a joke, wench." The woman pinched Dell's cheek. "It seems your mother couldn't afford to give you a smile neither." She let go of Dell's burning cheek. "I am Blanche, and you will smile at my patrons. And at my jests."

Dell busied herself, spreading clean rushes over the damp, dirty ones on the floor. While she dug through them, picking out unsavory bones and mouse carcasses, she uncovered a dirty trencher and a tankard. She glanced into the kitchen. Blanche's back was turned. Crawling under the bench, Dell licked at the gravy that had hardened on the trencher. Just as she picked up the tankard, the tavern door opened and two men stepped inside. She scrambled to her feet, ashamed to be seen scavenging like a beggar.

The taller of the two men was a pale fellow wearing a flat cap and an apron full of pockets. He looked like the man who'd talked to her yesterday ... yes ... it *was* him ... what was his name? ... John the Joiner? The men sat down at a table in the corner.

Dell hurried to the kitchen, filled two tankards with ale, and brought them to the table. She hoped the room was dim enough so John the Joiner wouldn't recognize her. Even though she kept her eyes lowered, she could feel him watching her. "Any bread or meat for you, sirs?"

The shorter man shook his head.

John took a great swallow of ale. "Well, well," he said.

"What a surprise. The rustic who can read."

Dell glanced up, but John's face held no look of surprise.

"So tell us," he went on, "do you know the meanings of words, or only the sounds?"

"A little," Dell whispered, remembering that word *traitor* on the handbill.

"Speak up, girl. A little what? A little sound? A little meaning?"

Too frightened to talk, she forced herself to smile as she'd been instructed to do.

John crooked his finger. "Come here."

Dell's chest tightened. She was certain there were no cannibals in the city, but still ... what if John grabbed her and took her for an amble?

He continued to smile, so Dell took a cautious step forward. Suddenly his hand shot out and seized her wrist.

"Please," she cried. "Let go." She twisted and pulled back, but he only held on more tightly. "Please." Her wrist throbbed.

Then he pressed something into her palm, closed her fingers around it, and let go. Dell stumbled backward. He leaned his forearms on the table and smiled. Dell did not smile back. Still, he had given her something.

She opened her hand. Three silver coins. Two were small and one was as big as her thumbprint. On the big coin was the face of a king. Her hands still trembled, but she turned the coins over, one by one.

"Shall I take these to Blanche?" she asked, her voice hoarse with fear.

"Only if you are a fool."

So the coins were for her. "Thank you."

Coins were important. If she had coins in her pocket, she wouldn't have to beg. If she was to survive in this city, she would have to learn about coins. If Margery were here right now she would explain everything. But Margery wasn't here. Dell had seen to that.

"Please," she said, holding out the coins. "What do you call these?"

John thumped his fist on the table and Dell jumped. "Why, filthy lucre, of course." Both men laughed and drank heartily from their tankards.

Dell's face burned. They were laughing at her, but at least they weren't threatening to eat her or chop off her head. "Are all three called lucres? Or have they different names?"

The men exchanged glances, but Dell didn't budge. She needed to know.

"Two halfpennies and a penny," said John. He leaned toward her and lowered his voice. "Don't forget. I am John the Joiner on Carpenter Lane. My blind father needs reading to."

The other man snorted.

"Have you a Bible?" Dell asked. "For reading?"

"A Bible. Ah, yes."

She clutched the coins. "I can't leave. I promised to work for Mistress Blanche."

"And Mistress Blanche, in return, promised to feed you, did she not?" John set down one more coin. "Payment for the ale." The two men rose and strode out the door.

As the morning wore on, the tavern grew noisier and the kitchen grew hotter. Dell ran back and forth with steaming bowls and trenchers. Sweat rolled down her face and stung her eyes. The patrons became increasingly drunk, and by noon she had been grabbed, pinched, squeezed, and petted.

At last twilight fell. Blanche pushed her remaining patrons out the door and bolted it shut. "I suppose you wants a place to sleep," she muttered. She nodded at the floor, set a plate of dry bread and cheese on a table, and clumped up the stairs to her room.

Exhausted, Dell collapsed on a bench and slipped Bartholomew onto her hand.

"Oh, Bartholomew," she sighed. "I thought I'd found us a place to live and work. But the patrons fondle me, and Blanche pays me in moldy cheese." She picked up the chunk of cheese and sniffed at it. "And not only that, but I'm no closer to Ronaldo than I was yesterday."

Bartholomew brushed a flea from his shoulder. "At least you have coins in your pocket. And John the Joiner has offered you a job." He crossed his arms over his chest. "But what of *me*? What of *my* desires? If you would let me be my true self, and not a mole in your pocket, I could help you earn a living."

"Fine. I'll carry you about for all the world to behold. Then we'll see how long you survive."

"Survive?" Bartholomew stuck his chin in the air. "In the public eye, I would thrive."

"You're wrong," Dell said. "This city is not a safe place." She curled up on a tabletop, using her arm as a pillow. Her body ached for something soft, but the rushes on the floor were crawling with vermin.

Sometime—in her fitful half-sleep—the dream came again. The man in the red vest juggling lemons. The lemons spinning faster and higher. The whinny of the horse. And then the scream—her own scream—jolting her awake.

After three days at the King's Head, Dell's body ached from the endless work and paucity of food. Her leggings had grown so loose that she had to cinch them tight to make them stay up. And she was no closer to the Boy now than when she'd arrived in the city.

At dawn on the fourth day, she was at the fire, boiling water in the cauldron.

Blanche thumped down the stairs. "Empty the chamber pot," she said in greeting. "Then I want you at the kneading trough." She unbolted the front door and opened the shutters.

Dell took in a great gulp of air. She'd had enough of this mean-spirited woman. The King's Head Tavern would not imprison her another night.

After Blanche had mixed the barley flour with ale, Dell washed her hands, pushed up her sleeves, and kneaded the mixture in the trough. Bartholomew lay heavy in her pocket, but she couldn't take him out now, not while her hands were sticky with dough.

A piece of spoiled mutton sat on the table. Its surface, which had turned a sickly, shimmering green, was crawling with tiny worms. Its odor had attracted a mangy dog, which crouched outside the kitchen door, drooling.

After Dell completed the kneading, she choked down her breakfast—dry bread, a half cup of ale, and a piece of sooty bacon that had fallen into the fire.

Blanche leaned over the mutton and sniffed. "Cut it into small pieces and throw it in the pot."

"But ... it's rotten."

Blanche picked up a knife and waggled it at Dell. "It's not King Henry we're cooking for, is it wench?" She raised the knife and thrust its point into the center of the meat.

Dell pulled the knife out of the mutton and began to saw through it. What if John the Joiner came in today and ate the spoiled meat? If he sickened from it, she would be to blame. She turned her head away from the rancid smell. The dog skulked in the doorway, strings of drool dangling from its mouth.

Blanche stood at the oven, her legs planted wide, balancing six rounds of dough on the huge bread paddle. She grunted with the effort.

Dell laid the blade of the knife flush with the side of the

meat and pushed it to the edge of the table. Blanche turned, just as the slab of mutton toppled onto the floor. Her face reddened in fury, but she didn't dare let go of the heavy paddle. The dog bounded into the room, and Dell ran.

CHAPTER

XIII

"Help!" Blanche shouted. "I've been robbed! Call the constable!"

Dell ducked around a corner and pressed her back against the wall. No footsteps pounded after her. No constable grabbed the neck of her smock. She breathed a sigh of relief.

But now what? How was she to find the Boy when she couldn't even tell one building from the next? The whole city was an ugly labyrinth of streets and alleys that all looked exactly the same.

On the mountain, she had followed the bright current of the stream or the worn path of a doe. By day she had been guided by the sun, and by night the stars. But here, the buildings leaned out so far into the street, she could hardly see the sky, much less the sun or the moon or the stars.

Out here on the street, at least she had a chance of finding the Boy. Even if he was promised to God, he could still tell her why he came up the mountain with the sack of supplies. But Ronaldo didn't even know who she was. Like Bartholomew had said, every time the Boy had come up the mountain, she'd hidden herself behind the roots of the fir tree. She walked past a wheelwright's and a barber's and a furrier's. Where *was* she?

Surely Ronaldo knew *something*. He had brought a chemise—just her size—up the mountain. And the pair of leggings she was wearing right now.

In the distance, the bells of St. Paul's rang out. Of course! Why hadn't she thought of it sooner? A point from which she could get her bearings. The towering steeple of the church. She hurried toward it.

She hadn't gone a hundred steps when the aroma of freshly baked bread enveloped her. A bakery. And in her pocket lay two halfpennies and a penny. From the window of the bakery protruded a shelf on which sat several round, fragrant loaves of brown bread. A number of women had queued along the wall. Dell's mouth watered.

The first woman in line pointed to a medium-sized loaf. "How much?" she said.

"A penny," the baker said with a scowl. "Same as yesterday."

"A penny!" the woman protested. "At Pie Corner, they sell me *two* loaves for a penny!" Still grumbling, she laid a coin on the shelf. Dell strained to see if the coin looked like hers, but the baker snatched it up and dropped it in his coffer before she could get a peek.

Dell joined the queue. A red-cheeked woman in front of her was talking about someone named Anne Boleyn, who had just been imprisoned in a tower.

"Adulterous whore," the woman said.

"Good riddance, that's what I say," said another. "The king will be well rid of her."

Dell stared down at her feet, straining to catch every word.

"A pity Catherine couldn't give him an heir. At least *she* is a decent woman."

Oh, yes, Dell longed to say. *She is more than decent. She taught my mother to read. She gave her a Bible.*

The red-cheeked woman glanced sideways at Dell, and the conversation turned to talk of slothful husbands and the high price of bread.

At last Dell's turn came. She held her breath and laid her penny on the shelf.

The baker swatted at a swarm of flies with his towel. "Medium or small?" he said.

The medium loaf was so steaming and beautiful, it shimmered. "Medium."

The baker took her penny. "Next," he said.

Dell reached out and grasped the loaf with both hands. No one screamed *thief* or *traitor*, so she hugged the hot bread to her bosom and hurried away. Her heart was still pounding, but she'd done it. She'd exchanged coins for food. Even Bartholomew would be pleased with her accomplishment.

Bartholomew. She still had not taken him out of her pocket as she had promised. But what did he expect? She couldn't very well tear off pieces of bread with a puppet on one hand. If only there were a stream where she could drink. She swallowed a chunk of bread, but a moment later her stomach cramped, causing her to double over.

She walked carefully, watching for puddles of animal blood, the spillage of chamber pots, pickpockets, and the steeple of St. Paul's all at the same time. The effort made her dizzy. Sometimes the steeple disappeared behind the slate roofs of homes and shops, but then it would suddenly appear in the gray sky and lead her forward. Nowhere did she see lemons for sale.

Nothing made sense in this city. Not the maze of streets nor the puzzle of people.

At least on the mountain she'd had a few things she could count on: the sun-warmed rocks and trees, the clear waters of the stream, the playful winking of the stars.

But most of all, Ronaldo.

Every time the moon had waned to its slenderest self, Ronaldo—the Brown Boy—had climbed faithfully up the mountain with his sack full of wonderful gifts. But Ronaldo, she now understood, was not just a solitary boy with a sack. He was—what had Margery said?—a novice in the Benedictine order of monks.

Monks. Saintly men who lived in monasteries. There were different kinds—*orders*—of monks, but they all had one thing in common. They gave themselves to God, not to women.

She thrust her hands into her pockets. Her left hand clutched Bartholomew, thank Heaven, and her right hand encircled the lemon. No, not the lemon. She had used the lemon to heal little Ned. She didn't regret that decision, but it saddened her to think of the lemon rind rotting in the gutter where Margery had tossed it. Dell kicked at a loose stone in the street. Her pocket contained not a lemon but a chunk of warm bread and two halfpennies. She hopped over a pile of slops and mud splattered her skirt.

When she finally found the square, it seemed even more crowded than the week before. Well, she didn't care. She would find Ronaldo—no matter what—and talk to him. Did he know, for instance, *why* he brought supplies up the mountain? Did he know about Lucretia? Could he tell her where the lemons came from?

She surveyed the square, her heart fluttering with both dread and longing.

Last week Ronaldo had been standing somewhere between the water conduit and St. Paul's, she was almost certain. But today, all she could see were a string of vendors, a minstrel playing a lute, and two crates of jittery rabbits. None looked like Ezekiel.

As she pushed her way across the square, she was jostled and grabbed and stepped on. She wove her way among the stalls, past the conduit, along the front wall of the church. Back and forth she walked. Again and again.

A plump monk strode past. "Indulgences," he shouted. He was ringing a silver bell and waving a handful of papers. "Buy your indulgences now before it is too late."

What was he talking about? Too late for what? Weary and weak, she sat down next to the church doors and leaned back against the smooth stones. The sun, unobstructed by shops and houses, spread its light across the square and warmed her face. She closed her eyes for just a moment.

A deep humming startled her awake. The sun had wandered off across the sky, leaving her in shadow. The stones of the church chilled her back, and the leg she'd been sitting on for so long had lost all feeling. She shivered. The low humming grew louder and reverberated inside her. She stood up to see what it was, and her leg prickled as it came back to life.

A procession of monks in black habits walked slowly, two by two, across the square. Their voices, united as one, droned a low repetitive song. No, not a song. A chant. They were chanting, like Auntie did at the grotto. Their chanting drifted over the peddlers and tinkers and housewives and rogues, and then settled, like a blessing, on Dell's ears.

Ronaldo wore a black habit, too, just like these men. Maybe he was a part of their order. The procession was coming this way. To St. Paul's.

They continued their slow, deliberate pace, seemingly unperturbed by the turmoil around them. The crowd, in fact, parted to make way for them as they crossed the square, a dark humming river of men. The drone of their voices soothed her and slowed her breathing—until the thought of seeing Ronaldo made her gasp for air.

The monks were so close now, Dell could make out a few of the words they were chanting. The words were in Latin, like the *Pater Noster* she had learned from Auntie. *Dimitii nostrum* meant "forgive us"; *benedicte* meant "blessed"; and *amen*, of course, meant "so be it." She wished she could see their features, but the men had pulled their cowls up over their heads, leaving their faces in mysterious shadow.

The first two monks approached the doors of the church. One of them swung a censer of incense. Its sweet, thick smoke filled the air, making it even more difficult to see the faces inside the cowls. Dell coughed and her eyes watered. Maybe this was the smoke that had drifted up to her on the mountain. Father had told her that the smoke came from unholy fires that roasted human flesh. But maybe it had risen from censers, like this one, that announced the presence of God.

The monks, barely an arm's length away, processed two by two into the church. Dell shrank back. Even if she *did* see Ronaldo, she couldn't just run to him. She would have to stand here and watch him go by. Well, so be it. Her eyes remained fastened on the dark procession passing before her. Her lips moved as she counted. Two ... four ... six. ... Black habits, black cowls, black capes. Twenty-six ... twenty-eight ...

Although all the monks looked agonizingly alike, some of their bodily features were distinct. Several had rotund bellies, and one was missing a hand. One monk was about Ronaldo's height, but his wide, swaying step told her that he was not Ronaldo. If only she could see their faces. Forty-two ... forty-four ... forty-six ...

She had all but given up hope when the second-to-last

pair of monks approached the door. One was uncommonly tall—a towering tree compared to Father—with stooped shoulders and a faltering gait. He was so thin, his habit seemed empty inside.

The other monk, younger and more robust, walked close to his frail partner, reaching out for the elderly man when he tilted or stumbled. As the pair passed through the doorway, the cowl of the younger monk turned, just for an instant, toward Dell. Her heart lurched, and a cry escaped from her lips.

XIV

It was Ronaldo! Dell was sure of it. And he had looked right at her. Hadn't he? The light of his eyes, the glimmer of his smile radiated through her. The pair of monks disappeared into the darkness of the church, and the brief light that had flickered inside Dell sputtered out.

No. Her mind was playing tricks. If he had seen her, he would have nodded or saluted her. "Dell!" he would have called out. "Ho, there! Dell!" Nonsense. How could he call to her? He didn't know her name. Did he?

Maybe it wasn't even him. She crossed her arms over her smock and paced back and forth along the wall of the church. The minutes dragged by. Church bells pealed. People came and went through the thick wooden doors. Well, if the monks weren't coming out, there was only one thing to do.

She grabbed the heavy metal ring on the door and pulled with all her might. The door swung slowly open. Dell blinked in the musty dimness. The inside of the church was as crowded and noisy as the street. But Dell wasn't looking at the swarm of people at the back of the church. Her gaze rose up, higher and higher. She gasped in amazement.

The ceiling of this church was so high and so vaulted, it

looked like the dome of Heaven. And all around her, angels and archangels flew on exquisite wings that sparkled in patterns of colored light.

On the front wall of the church, behind a great altar, a cross had been raised, and on the cross hung the Savior. Blood dripped from his side and the crown of thorns bowed his suffering head.

Awed and horrified, Dell fell to her knees. Her hair brushed the floor. "Lord Jesus Christ, have mercy on me," she prayed. She glanced up. Neither Jesus nor the angels had moved a muscle. Dell's face grew hot. What a simpleton she was.

Jesus was a statue, and the colorful angels were part of the windows that ran the length of the church. She had never imagined anything so magnificent. She was still kneeling on the cold floor when the smell of stale piss settled over her. Something tugged at her skirt and she turned her head, startled. A woman's face hovered close to hers. Dell covered her nose and mouth in order to breathe.

The woman's cheeks were pale and hollow, but her eyes smoldered. Both her hands were planted on the floor and she was leaning forward on them, swaying to the droning music of the chant. Knotted cords of gray hair hung over her shoulders and swayed back and forth with her.

"Alms for a cripple."

Of course. This was the same woman who had sat outside the gate, the one whose legs were cut off at the knees.

Dell tried to stand, but the woman picked up one arm

and brought it down, *thump*, on Dell's skirt. Then she did the same with her other arm, pinning Dell to the spot where she knelt.

The woman smiled, showing her remaining teeth. "You remember me, don't you?" She smelled like Blanche's slab of spoiled meat. "The nuns, God bless them, be moving me here. I be earning more alms in a church."

"*Earning?* You have *earned* nothing." Dell tried to pull back, but the woman's hands were pegs, nailing Dell's skirt to the floor. If she stood up, she would cause the woman to topple over and roll across the floor like a log. Sickened, Dell turned her head to one side.

"You and I, we are the same." The woman sneered. She pulled up her skirt to show Dell her stumps. One of them oozed with pus.

A sharp sourness rose in Dell's throat. "That's gibberish," she said. But what if the woman spoke the truth? Here in the city, Dell wasn't a part of anything. She was no one. Beads of sweat rolled down her temples. She dug into her pocket and threw down one of her halfpennies. As long as she had something to give, no one could call her a beggar. The coin clinked on the stone floor.

The woman shifted all her weight to one arm, snatched up the coin, and bit down on it with her mossy teeth. "Ask and it shall be given you." She lifted her remaining hand off Dell's skirt, and Dell, unanchored, sprang to her feet. Her hands were cold and sweaty. The woman's words echoed in her head. *We are the same.* The woman was mad, *mad*. Dell turned and stumbled into a rag seller and several geese.

The monks, meanwhile, had divided into two bodies—half on one side of the church and half on the other—facing one another. Their monotonous drone was like the rolling murmur of the stream, drowning out the hubbub around her. Dell wrapped her arms around her trembling body and took heart, knowing Ronaldo was close by.

Guilt choked her. Here she stood, in the presence of the suffering Christ, dreaming about the lips and eyes of Ronaldo. *Kyrie eleison*. Christ have mercy.

The next thing she knew, the monks were shuffling past her, two by two, toward the door of the church. In a moment Ronaldo would be so close she would be able to reach out and touch his black habit. She might be able to see his mischievous smile, his crooked nose. She squinted at the men as they passed by. But the church was so dark, she couldn't tell one monk from another. They blurred into one long and pious body. And in a moment they would be gone.

Angels hovered everywhere, their innocent eyes beaming with adoration for the Savior. Why couldn't she be like them? "Kyrie. ..."

A cough from a passing monk interrupted her prayer, and she looked up. His cowl had fallen back, exposing a dark face surrounded by a mass of straight, brown hair. The room seemed suddenly bright, and she could see his lips, his crooked nose, his velvet eyes. ...

Ronaldo didn't turn his head, but his gaze lighted on her like an angel's wing. His upturned lips were a sliver of moon. She blinked, and when she opened her eyes, the cowl was back over his head, the figure had moved past and he was gone—a dream that had never happened.

But it *had* happened. Ronaldo had smiled at her. Maybe—somehow—he *did* know who she was. Now all she had to do was follow him to the monastery where he lived, talk to him, ask him ... ask him what? Her mouth was dry with excitement and fear.

When the last monk had filed past, Dell turned to follow him. The spark that had shone in Ronaldo's eyes was a bright torch lighting her way. Her heart thumped in her chest. From a dim corner in the back of the church came a high-pitched snigger. The beggar woman was laughing at her and her foolish desires.

Dell reached into her pocket. Bartholomew. Her dear, fuzzy-headed friend. Even if no one else knew her, he did. Why, he even had a scheme for the both of them to earn a living. Dell followed along in the protective wake of the procession, grateful not to be buffeted by the pushing and shoving of the crowds.

She shuffled along unfamiliar streets and byways, never more than a few paces behind the last pair of monks. For awhile, a great white horse followed behind the procession, too. She turned and glanced up. On the creature's back sat the same man she'd seen one other time—the man with the ermine-trimmed hat and the sagging jowls. He looked so haughty and powerful up there, she felt relieved when he turned the horse and went a different direction.

At last they arrived at what must be the monastery, although all that was visible was a high stone wall with a massive door. Another monk stood inside the door, holding it open for his returning brothers. His cowl was pushed back, revealing a bald and scabby pate. Dell edged closer to the door, her heartbeat quickening. When the last pair of monks had passed into the monastery grounds, the scabby-headed monk leaned against the door, and it began to swing shut.

"Wait!" Dell cried. She rushed toward him, stepping on the skirts of a beggar woman as she ran.

The monk paused, looking Dell up and down. "If you seek lodging, you will have to go elsewhere. The free beds for beggars are full."

Dell sucked in her breath. "I am not a beggar."

"A traveler then?" The monk raised one eyebrow. "Not alone, I pray." He leaned past the door, peering first in one direction and then in the other. "If you are traveling with father or husband or brother, and have means to pay, we have three beds remaining."

"No," said Dell. "That's not why I came. I came because. ..." Her tongue thickened in her mouth, and she looked down at her feet. In the street sat a frail and dirty woman. And beside her, a little girl with spindly arms. When the little girl smiled up at Dell, spittle ran out the corner of her mouth.

Dell averted her eyes. Everywhere she went she saw beggars, and she was sick to death of them all. The monk coughed impatiently.

Dell swallowed the dry lump in her throat. Her chance was slipping away. "I came to see Ronaldo," she blurted out.

The monk leaned on the door. "Ronaldo has no sister. Only a brother, Tomás. A traveling merchant from across the sea." He looked Dell up and down again, his eyes condemning every rip in her skirt, every stain on her bodice. She licked the back of her hand and rubbed it across her cheek.

"I recognize you," the monk said, and for an instant Dell's spirit took wings. The monk knew who she was!

"You are Eve." He looked with disdain at the beggar woman in the street, then back at Dell. "The both of you. Eve and Eve."

Dell shrank back. "No. I am Dell."

"It is you who ate of the apple and brought sin into the world."

"I didn't. ..." But then she thought about the lemon. It *had* tempted her—just as the apple had tempted Eve—and now look where she was. In a city rife with wickedness.

"You are the coy and wheedling temptress, come to this holy place to prey upon our weakest members. Of course it is Ronaldo you seek. Of course. Fair-faced, sweet-voiced Ronaldo."

"Please—"

The monk's eyes were two slits and his voice was a hiss. "But Brother Gregory, you see, will never allow it. He protects the boy from evil. Do you understand?" Before Dell could utter a word of protest, he heaved the door shut in her face.

"Please." She pounded on the shiny wood until her fist grew red and sore. "Please." She threw her shoulder against the door, then kicked it with her foot.

"A foul one, he be," said the beggar woman beside Dell.

Startled, she stopped pounding and glanced down.

"Even his farts be dreadful rotten," the woman continued. Her body jerked forward, as if someone had kicked her from behind. "The other monks—the almoners—they be giving us bread or a bit of boiled fish. Tomorrow we be getting better luck, you'll see." She smiled weakly and patted the ground beside her. "Come, sit with us."

"I—I can't." Dell took a step back, a step that would put space between her and this sickly woman. A space that would say to Dell, *I am not a helpless beggar like you.*

The woman went on. "Did he be your sweetheart then, Ronaldo?"

Sweetheart. The very word sent a wave of heat coursing up Dell's neck and across her cheeks. Her neck prickled.

The woman seemed to notice Dell's embarrassment. "I pray you didn't whore yourself."

"No," Dell choked.

"Praise God. Because if you be bearing the child of a monk, you be bearing it alone."

"He's not a monk," Dell stammered. "Not yet."

"You looks like a good girl. Would you do a dying woman a final kindness?"

Dell reached into her pocket, took out a chunk of bread, and thrust it into the woman's hands. "Here, then."

"P-f-f-f-t. What do bread provide, except another day of earthly sorrow?" The woman gave the bread to the spindly-armed girl, then withdrew a coin from her bodice. "What I asks you to do is this—I gots one penny, I do. Take it and buy me an indulgence."

"An indulgence?" Dell asked. Hadn't the friar outside St. Paul's been selling indulgences? "Is it some kind of remedy?"

"A remedy, yes, but not for the body. It be a remedy for the *soul!* It be a pardon from sin." The woman's cheeks flushed and she talked faster now. "Friar Julius be selling them in the square. He gots a silver coffer, and on it be two angels—Master Cherubim and Mistress Seraphim. And he be ringing a little silver bell. The indulgence be a ticket out of the sufferings of purgatory. Out of purgatory and into Heaven. Surely you be hearing him sing his pretty rhyme in the square?"

Dell's eyes widened with astonishment. "The friar sells forgiveness of sins?"

"Indeed he do." The woman bowed her head. "Brother Gregory be saying I ought to keep my penny. He be saying the friar is a thief. Still, if it aren't too much trouble. ..."

"I'll do what I can." Dell took the woman's penny. This

beggar was kind and gentle, so different from that foul stump-legged woman. Dell broke the remaining bread into three portions. The woman ignored hers, so the little girl gobbled down both shares. Dell forced down a bite, but a moment later she experienced such a sharp cramp that she gave the last bite to the little girl. The child, who appeared to lack speech, gurgled her thanks.

Dell's body ached, and the thickening mist made her shiver. She summoned up all her strength and banged on the monastery door one more time. But it had closed against her, and no amount of kicking or pounding would open it.

CHAPTER

XV

Before she could do anything— anything at all—she needed water. Her lips were cracked and her gait unsteady. She could almost taste the water that poured from the conduit in the square, sweet and clean and cold as the water that burbled in the stream. She gave the monastery door one last kick and trudged back the way she had come.

The steeple of St. Paul's, when it was visible, led her forward. The roofs of buildings leaned over the streets, blocking out the light of the sun, and the patches of sky that remained were sullied by smoke and soot. Whether it was noon or dusk, she couldn't be sure.

When she reached the square, even the sky was a dull expanse of gray. The sun, hidden in dark clouds, cast no shadows that would indicate the time of day. And although the air had grown cool and misty, Dell's cheeks felt hot.

Two water carriers stood by the conduit, their backs bent under the weight of their casks. Dell rushed past them to the spigot, opened her mouth, and gulped greedily. The water streamed over her lips and tongue and down her throat. It ran through her matted tangle of hair and down her burning face.

A moment later her head flew up and she spat out the

water in a violent spray. She sputtered and spat again. The water wasn't clear and cold. It was warm and foul and it stank of rot and offal. Dell spat and wiped her lips and spat again.

One of the water carriers uttered a great guffaw and pointed at Dell with his thumb. "A mad dog, that one. See the foam at its mouth."

The other carrier lifted his leg next to the conduit—in imitation of a pissing dog. He barked, then howled at the dark sky. "A mangy cur."

"A worthless bitch."

As Dell stumbled away, a drop of rain fell on her cheek. Then another and another. Her gut twinged. All around her, the vendors were closing up their stalls. There was a crack of thunder and the rain fell in earnest. She needed shelter. She slipped and slid along street after muddy street. Streams of water rushed over her shoes. Where did John the Joiner say he lived? Carpenter Lane?

If only she had stayed with Margery. But she couldn't. She wasn't a part of her family. Even when she had been inside their house, the real Dell had stood outside it, looking in.

Her belly cramped, and she winced at the pain of it. Rain ran down her neck. It penetrated her smock and made her shoulders chilly and damp. As her skin turned colder, her gut flamed hotter. The cramps in her belly grew stronger, angrier, until they erupted in a searing pain that bent her body in half.

She straightened her body and walked on, the rain

pelting her. Her woolen skirt was so weighted with water, it made every step a labor. Her wet leggings chafed against her thighs, and her teeth clacked. She retched but had nothing to expel. The rain fell relentlessly. Her fingers had turned to ice but her eyes burned. All around her people were shouting and scurrying. Doors slammed, shutters banged. Everyone was going home.

The bells of St. Paul were ringing—had been ringing—what? None? Matins? The day must be nearly spent. With every peal, her head throbbed. Margery had warned her that if she walked the streets after curfew, she'd be picked up by the night watch and thrown into prison. She and Bartholomew both.

Poor Bartholomew. She tried to wriggle her hand into her pocket but her fingers were stiff with cold. She stumbled headfirst into a man with a chest as hard as wood. His face was shaven, and he was wearing a flat cap like the one John the Joiner had worn at the King's Head Tavern.

Maybe he *was* John the Joiner. But his face was so blurry. Everything was blurry. Even the buildings wobbled. Maybe she could work for him after all, read to his blind father, earn her keep.

Her teeth chattered so hard, she could barely speak. "John the Joiner?" she said.

"Can't hear you," the man shouted over the rain. No. No, it wasn't him at all.

"I—I'm looking for John the Joiner. On Carpenter Lane."

"Carpenter Lane?" the man boomed. "Not far." He pointed along the street. "Just past Butcher's Row. You'll smell *that* soon enough." He pulled his cape close and rushed on, his boots squelching through the mud.

She leaned into the wind. Shop signs, hidden behind the curtain of rain, swayed and creaked. She plodded on, her body trembling and burning. She couldn't see through the downpour but she could smell everything. Butcher's Row.

She struggled through a gray tunnel of rain, guided by the lowing of cows. Bloody guts swirled around her feet and rushed past her in dark rivulets of water. Her legs swayed like reeds.

Fever, chills, retching—of course—she'd been struck down by the pestilence. She would die on the streets like a beggar, and her death wouldn't matter to anyone. What a fool she'd been—to think she could survive in this city. She staggered on, past the blood and stench and moaning of doomed animals.

When she looked up, everything—shutters and roofs, carts and wagons—everything was wheeling around her head. She stumbled toward the nearest door, but her knees buckled. Drops of rain sparkled like stars. She reached out with flailing arms and the spinning world went black.

Dell opened her eyes. Where was she? She touched her brow and winced at the tender lump. It must be a pustule, a sign of the pestilence. Above her was a low, sloping ceiling, and spread across it was the giant shadow of Ezekiel—his two long ears, his whiskers, even the white patch behind his eye. But Ezekiel was dead. Maybe she had died, too, and gone to Heaven. She raised a leaden arm but it fell back with a thump.

The next time she opened her eyes, the light around her had paled. Somewhere close by two men were talking.

"How now, John?" the one voice said with a laugh. "Whose skirt hangs in your shop?"

Dell sucked in her breath. That voice! It wasn't a man's. It was Ronaldo's, she was certain.

"It is not what it appears," said John. "A girl collapsed outside my door Tuesday last. Burning with fever. She's a rustic, but she can read. She was working at the King's Head, and no doubt Blanche drove her to the point of illness."

"The girl's eyes?" said Ronaldo. "Are they a pale violet—like the last shades of day?"

Despite her weakness, Dell raised her head. How could

Ronaldo know the color of her eyes? He'd never even *seen* her.

"I have seen this girl," Ronaldo continued. "Brother Gregory sends me on errands of mercy into her region. I have watched her slip among the trees, shy as a fox."

Dell's face grew hot and she threw back the sheet.

"But here's the queerest thing," said John. "Look what fell from her pocket."

Her pocket! Dell's hands fumbled for Bartholomew, but her fingers touched only her chemise. Her skirt and smock and leggings were gone. She was nearly naked, and Bartholomew was gone. John had stolen him. She let out a moan.

"So the girl is a puppeteer, like her mother," said Ronaldo. "She's an enchanting creature. Were I an unwed man, like you—"

John laughed. "You *are* an unwed man, my boy, and methinks you have pondered on this girl rather much for a monk."

"What I mean is—if you had a wife, she could keep your larder stocked and the coals warm."

"You know why the fire is cold." John's voice grew suddenly stern. "I shan't marry a woman only to turn her into a widow. Tell me now, what word. ..." He lowered his voice, and the conversation became a mumble.

Dell touched the lump on her head again and closed her eyes. "Oh, Bartholomew," she whispered.

All around her the lemons again, spinning higher and higher. The whinny of a horse. A crash. She was trying to run, but she was trapped—tangled in something. She fought to escape. The next thing she knew, someone was prying open one of her eyelids. She jerked her head to one side.

A hand slid behind her head and raised it. "Girl," said the voice of John the Joiner. "You need to drink." He was nudging the rim of a wooden cup between her lips. "And untangle yourself from the sheet."

Dell blinked and looked over his shoulder. Ronaldo was nowhere in sight. When had she last heard his voice? An hour ago? A week? Had she dreamt him?

"Come now," John said. "I am unlearned in the womanly art of nursing. If you do not do your part and open your mouth, you will be dead by curfew."

The shadow of Ezekiel stretched across the ceiling. No, not a shadow. Just a stain that had taken on the shape of a rabbit.

Dell turned her head away from the cup. "The water in this city is foul."

"Of course it is. But this is a caudle that my neighbor, Goodwife Culpepper, made for you. It will restore you."

She took a sip. It didn't taste like any of Auntie's remedies, or like the honey and lemon mixture her mother had once given to her. But it tasted far better than the dredge from the conduit. And she was so thirsty. She tried to raise herself on her elbows, but her body was too heavy. "I can earn my keep," she managed to say. "I can read to your father."

"My father?" John said. "Ah, yes, my father. He is at the home of his sister this week." He encouraged her to take another sip. "Have you a tattling tongue?"

She stuck it out so he could examine it and decide for himself.

"What I mean is, are you a clucking hen? A gossip?"

Her head pounded, and the whiskers of the rabbit above her twitched. These questions were tricky. And then suddenly it came to her, and her body gave a little jerk—she was lying in the bed of a man she didn't know—a man who had stolen her clothing and Bartholomew—and she was too weak to move. Well, she had best tell him one thing she *wasn't*. "I am not a whore."

The cup slipped in John's hands and a few drops splashed into her eye. He dabbed at it with a corner of the sheet. "A good thing," he said. "The city has quite a plenty of them already. But if not a whore, then what?"

What indeed? "I'm a puppeteer, and you have stolen my puppet. I demand that you—"

John leaned over and set the cup on the floor. When he straightened up, he had hold of Bartholomew and was trying to force his large fingers into the sleeves of the puppet's harlequin suit.

"Don't," she cried. "You'll rip it."

He handed Bartholomew to Dell. "You must show me the proper way."

Dell breathed a sigh of relief. John hadn't stolen him after all. "Like this." She slipped Bartholomew onto her hand, and the puppet stood beside her, smiling protectively.

"You must have run away from a family of entertainers."

"I need to go." Dell raised herself up on her elbows, but her arms collapsed, and she flopped back onto the mattress. She had to go now—right now—in case the pustules had spread all over her body. No one would allow a victim of the pestilence out on the streets. She touched the lump on her forehead and winced. "Are they everywhere?"

"They?" John the Joiner looked over his shoulder, then leapt up and hurried to the window. "Who do you mean, *they*?"

"The pustules. Have they spread?"

He sat back down, and a long whistly breath escaped from his lips. "That lump is from the night you collapsed at my door. And your clothes are—"

Dell yanked up the blanket. "How dare you take my clothes!"

"Peace. It's not what you think. It was not I, but Goodwife Culpepper who tended to you. She washed your clothing and it's drying now, down in the shop. And she put in a cap for you as well."

Dell tucked the blanket all around herself and watched him warily. "How can you be sure the lump is not a pustule?"

John shrugged. "Spring is not the ripest season for the pestilence. It will come later, with the vapors of summer."

He tipped the cup to her mouth again. His thumb was black and rotten-looking. She pointed at it. "Then what is *that,* if not a pustule?"

"This?" He held up the hideous thumb. "My hammer hit me. Seven years of apprenticeship and ten years in my own shop, and still my hammer defies me."

The longer John the Joiner sat beside her, the more her head throbbed and the more confused she became. He had given her coins, and now a warm bed, a soothing drink, and gentle words. He'd made her feel comfortable, as if she belonged here. On the other hand, he had possession of her skirt and leggings and shoes.

He stroked Bartholomew's fuzzy head with his blackened thumb. "A puppet needs a stage, does it not?"

A stage. Dell tried to clear her head. A stage was exactly what Bartholmew wanted. But what about her—Dell? Did she want a stage, too? She *had* taken pleasure in performing for Margery's little brother, Ned. She nodded hesitantly.

"A puppet, you see, could say things in the public square that a man could not." John went to the window again and looked down onto the street. "Have you taken the Oath of Allegiance to the king?"

Now she was more confused than ever. She knew what an oath was—Father swore oaths all the time—but she had never heard the word *allegiance.* Maybe if she waited, John would explain what the Oath of Allegiance had to do with puppet stages.

"King Henry, for instance, would not behead a puppet

for treason." He looked at Bartholomew and smiled.

Dell did not smile. At the word *treason*, her voice shrank to a whisper. "But the king could take the head of the puppeteer, could he not?"

"Aye," John sighed, "there is that."

XVII

A week passed before Dell was strong enough to stand. John helped her walk downstairs to his workshop. She needed to go back to the monastery with an indulgence for the kindly beggar woman, but she barely had the strength to shuffle to the chamber pot. She settled herself on the bench and pulled her blanket around her shoulders. Thank Heaven John wasn't prattling on about the Oath of Allegiance. Dell swirled her toes through the cushion of sawdust and shavings on the floor, listening for his father's footsteps.

The shop was full of tools and partially completed chests and stools and chairs. She wondered if John finished building things or if he left his half-built furniture to rot, the way Father did. The hammers and saws looked familiar enough—Father owned one of each—but the rest of the tools were foreign to her.

The chisel, John explained, had a flat blade for shaping wood. The adz had a thin, arched blade for forming curves. "And here is the plane." He pushed the metal tool along a pine board, smoothing off the last nub of a knot hole. The scent of pine reminded her of sunny afternoons on the mountain. If she were there now, she would be breathing in the scents of newly blossomed flowers.

John pointed out the different kinds of wood in the room. He pulled a board from behind a chest and held it up to the light. Ash, he said, might be a good choice for a stage, because it was light. Oak and hornbeam—they were excellent woods—but too heavy to carry about. "And of course," he went on, "your stage will require joints, and that is my chiefest skill. Dovetail joints." His eyes shone as he spoke about his trade, and even though Dell had never heard of a dovetail joint, she knew he was talking sense.

He set before her two smooth pieces of wood that, when brought together, formed a corner, or what he called a *dovetail*. The joining looked a little like interlocking knuckles. One board had square notches cut into it and the other had sticking-out squares that fit snugly between the notches of the other board. "See," he said proudly, tugging them apart. "A perfect joint for a stage that will many times be assembled and disassembled."

For a moment Dell imagined herself inside a real puppet booth, hidden behind a colorful curtain—maybe red or blue—while a large crowd gathered to watch Bartholomew perform. If she had a puppet stage, she could become a real puppet master. The thought sent a pleasant shiver up her backbone. But a stage required more than wood. "I have no cloth for a curtain," she said. "But if I could begin reading to your father, I could earn enough money to buy some."

"And read you shall," John said as he dug through a box of wooden pegs. He held up two that matched. "We'll need a quantity of these, too."

"When can I begin reading?"

"Why, when he returns from his sister's. We will need a straight and sturdy timber for the curtain rod. Willow if the curtain is light, or hickory if it requires something sturdier. Be on the lookout."

"I will." She looked around the room. "Where do you keep your Bible?"

"My Bible." He set down the pegs and looked around, too. "You must be a good Christian, then. Are you?"

Dell's back stiffened and she wriggled to the edge of the bench. She thought of her ugly feelings toward the crippled beggar woman. "I try to be—but I often fail."

He continued to pick pegs out of the box, but his hands began darting and grabbing now. "And do you believe that the Pope is the head of the Christian church on earth?"

"Yes, of course," Dell whispered. She slid along the bench to be closer to the door. "Who else *could* be?"

"Who else, indeed!" John flung a handful of pegs at the wall.

Dell jumped, and the blanket fell from her shoulders.

The pegs scattered across the floor. "Our good king, perhaps? Upheld by that devil, Cromwell?"

Dell gripped the bench. What was he talking about?

John dragged his fingers through his strawlike mop of hair. "Look what I have done," he said in a quieter voice. "I have caused an invalid girl to cower in my own home." He knelt down and crawled through the sawdust, picking up the pegs one by one. "I have seen enough cowering these days. Priests and monks and nuns afraid for their very lives." He picked up the blanket that had slipped off Dell's shoulders and laid it on the bench beside her. "Forgive me."

Dell pulled the blanket close. John was talking nonsense. She'd watched the monks processing to St. Paul's, and they hadn't acted afraid. But then she thought of the plundered church with its smashed windows. Surely priests had worked there. When the church was ransacked, what had happened to them? Where had they gone? Maybe she would inquire another time, when she felt stronger and John was of a more sensible mind.

A few days later Dell persuaded John—against his better judgment—to allow her to go out. It was Friday, a fast day, and they would need fish from the market, would they not? John was in the shop, sawing a board. "If any be passing out handbills, take some." He reached absently into his purse and gave Dell a handful of coins.

In her hand lay one penny and a larger coin she didn't recognize. She asked John what it was worth, so she wouldn't be swindled.

He laid down his saw. "That? Why, a sixpence. It's equal to six pennies."

"Enough for six indulgences, then?"

"Indulgences?" John raised his eyebrows. "They're nothing but foolery."

"I promised to buy one from Friar Julius—for a dying beggar woman."

He laid three more tiny coins on the bench. "These are farthings. Give *them* to the beggars. And don't forget the handbills."

Dell thanked him and left. But handbills? No, she wanted nothing more to do with them.

The square was crowded—it must be a market day—and the never-ending shouts of *What do you lack? What do you need?* nearly drove Dell back to the house. She didn't feel as strong as she had that morning lying on her bed. But she had to keep her promise to the beggar woman. And maybe see Ronaldo. She pushed her way through the crowd, straining to hear the friar's silver bell.

A moment later, over the bleating of sheep and the honking of geese, she heard the delicate tinkle of bells. There, next to the water conduit, stood an upside-down dwarf wearing a red hat that tied under his chin. From the point of the hat hung a cluster of tiny bells. The man was walking on his hands and at the same time rolling a fire stick on the underside of his feet. Beside him walked a woman who was even shorter than he.

Had Father once juggled a fire stick like this one—maybe in this very same spot? Had Lucretia followed his act with a puppet show? *The past is done,* Father had said. But maybe the past was standing in front of her, right now, juggling fire. Dell hurried on.

The next bell she heard belonged to Friar Julius. He

stood near the church door, his silver money box under his arm. His body was round as a ball of dough, and his puffy cheeks jiggled when he shook his bell.

He waved a handful of papers and sang out, "When a penny in the coffer rings, another soul from purgatory springs."

Dell held out a penny to him. "One, please."

But Friar Julius looked right over Dell's head. She turned. Behind her stood a man wearing a cloak of brown velvet. On his head he wore a matching velvet cap with a feather in it.

Friar Julius bumped Dell aside with his belly. "My child," he said to the man, "I can tell you are a good son. No doubt you provide well for your mother and your father. But answer me this." He tugged on the gauntlet of the man's glove. "Have you provided for their eternal souls?"

The man pulled off his white glove, one finger at a time. His face looked solemn.

"For only one shilling," the friar continued, "you can release your mother and father from one hundred years of suffering in purgatory."

The man slipped his hand into his purse and withdrew a silver coin that was bigger than Dell's sixpence. And shinier.

"And for a crown," the friar continued, "you can release them for five hundred years. Think on it. *Five hundred years*. For only one crown."

The man frowned, but he dropped the shilling back in

his purse and withdrew a gold coin. Friar Julius smiled as the crown clinked in his coffer.

Dell pushed her way in front of the friar. "Father. I have a penny. I need an indulgence for a dying woman."

He leaned close and pinched her cheek so hard, she gasped. "God bless you, child," he said loudly. He gave her a shove and pressed forward into the crowd.

"Father, please," Dell called. She followed him for awhile, but he walked with haste, shouting out his rhyme.

"Thief." Dell clutched the woman's penny. "John was right. You're nothing but a thief." Now she would have to return to the beggar woman, empty-handed.

As she headed toward the monastery, she passed the dwarf, who was still juggling sticks of fire. His wife held out his pointy cap with its tinkling bells and Dell dropped in a farthing.

CHAPTER

XVIII

When Dell arrived at the monastery, the mute girl with the crooked arms sat alone at the gate, spittle dribbling from her lips.

Dell looked anxiously along the wall, then turned to the girl. "The woman who sat beside you? Do you know where she's gone?"

The child gurgled something, then raised her eyes Heavenward.

"So I've come too late," Dell groaned. "Do you think her sins were so great that God would condemn her to an eternity in purgatory?" The girl waggled her head, and Dell laid the unspent penny in the child's lap.

As the girl smiled in thanks, the monastery door creaked open. Dell leapt to one side, bracing herself for the scabby-headed monk and his hateful insults.

A different monk—a tall, frail one—appeared. He eased himself out the door, his hand groping along the wall. Something about his awkward appearance made Dell smile.

No two parts of him matched. His shiny head was too small for his towering body, his sticking-out ears were too large for his head, and his hands were too broad and thick for his gangly arms.

His milky eyes and then his body wandered toward the beggar child. He patted the air several times before his hand finally landed gently on the girl's head. "God be with you, child," he said. How could he stand to touch her lice-ridden hair? The girl jerked forward. "Have we something for this beautiful child of God?"

For a moment Dell thought he was addressing the question to her—no one else was close by—and then she turned. Oh, Heavenly powers! It was Ronaldo. He stood in the doorway, holding a large basket. He was grinning right at her.

"Ronaldo," said the elderly monk, "do you hear me?"

"One moment, Brother Gregory. I'm finding the choicest bun." Dell's cheeks grew hot, her gut churned. But what alarmed her most was the throbbing in her groin—a symptom she hadn't experienced during her confinement—as if her life blood was pulsing through her hidden parts. Maybe she was succumbing to the pestilence after all. And just when she was face to face with Ronaldo. She wanted to cry out to him—to explain who she was and why she had come. But the words that came out of her mouth were from the Song of Solomon—the ones he had recited on the mountain. "The winter is past," she said. "The rain is over and gone." Had she gone mad?

Brother Gregory turned toward the sound of Dell's voice. He squinted, as if to clear his cloudy eyes, and then he smiled. "Lucretia, is that you?" he asked. "Come. I will get you lemons to sell in the square. You know what a pretty price they bring." His large hand moved through the air, searching for her, and then lightly touched her cheek. "No, no, what an old fool I am. Lucretia is in the arms of God."

Dell's mouth fell open. The old monk had mistaken her for her mother.

"She's Lucretia's daughter," Ronaldo said. "She's Odelia."

"Can it be?" said Brother Gregory. "Praise God."

"But I'm not Odelia," Dell said. "I'm Dell."

"But you were christened Odelia." Brother Gregory smiled. "Welcome, child. I did not think to meet you again in this life."

Dell bit down on her lip. Father and Auntie had never called her Odelia, and yet the name felt as if it belonged to her. Dell was a fine enough name—sturdy and solid, like a brick. But Odelia was music—like the song of the stream tumbling down the mountain. Odelia. Would she have to choose who she was? Or could she be both Dell *and* Odelia?

Dell. Odelia. The names clashed inside her and she listed to one side. Ronaldo sprang to his feet to steady her. His hand, warm and strong, surrounded her wrist, and she sucked in her breath. If she didn't move or breathe, if they both stood as still as marble statues, if they both *became* statues, then this moment would go on and on, they would stay like this, melded together, touching one another, through all the rest of their lives, on and on, just the two of them, into the farthest, deepest reaches of eternity.

"I—I'm all right," she said and pulled back her hand. "Can you tell me more about my family—how we came to our mountain?"

"Your mountain?" Ronaldo threw back his head and laughed. "Your *mountain* is naught but a hill."

Dell's cheeks grew warm. "Can you tell me how we came to live on our *hill*?"

Brother Gregory laid a hand on Ronaldo's shoulder. "Odelia—hasn't your father ever explained to you—"

"My father has only told me that this is a city where men eat each other's flesh and drink each other's blood."

Brother Gregory sighed. "And so he believes, poor soul. He still lives in the clutches of his grief ... and shame, I suppose, that he could not save her."

"But Auntie told me that Father *did* save Lucretia."

"And so he did—the first time, when he helped her to escape the palace."

Ronaldo pulled away from the elder monk. "She wounded the king's pride, so he ordered her to be murdered."

Murdered? Why would anyone murder her mother? And yet even Bartholomew had questioned the circumstances of Lucretia's death. "So my mother's death was not an accident?"

A low growl rose from Ronaldo's throat.

"That is not ours to judge," said the elder monk. "Only God knows what was in the king's heart. And the soldier's. But we thought it best for your family to leave the city. I expected them to return after awhile, but. ..."

Murdered. The word drowned out every other sound. It dammed up the flood of questions inside her.

"Tell me," Brother Gregory continued, "what brings you here from the hills? Is your family in good health?" He gave Ronaldo's ear a gentle tweak. "Has this good novice been stealing necessities from the sack? Not the lemons, I pray?"

"Oh, no—that is, yes—my family is well. Thanks to the gifts we receive in the sack. But I don't live on the mountain—the *hill*—anymore. I live here now—at the house of John the Joiner. I work for him. That is, I will begin working for him very soon. Tomorrow, I hope."

The elderly monk took a deep breath.

"Look, Brother," Ronaldo said, "Odelia's skin grows pale."

"Help the girl to John's then, but don't tarry. And buy parsley on your way." Brother Gregory shook his head. "We grow our own, of course, but this boy—he sits by the garden at eventide and allows the rabbits to eat every sprig. Even after he has been whipped for it—thrice."

"All God's creatures must eat," Ronaldo said.

Brother Gregory made little clucking noises. "The boy should have been a Franciscan."

Ronaldo held out his hand to Dell. She stared at the open palm, at the encouraging fingers and the helpful thumb, all hovering in front of her, beckoning her to come. When she didn't move, he reached out and took her hand in his.

She stumbled forward and her breasts bumped into his

chest. She jumped back, as if her bosom had just caught fire. "Forgive me," she said. And then the fire settled into a heat so radiant, it warmed her through and through.

Her hand in his. Their hands together. And in between them, the damp and gritty crumbs of bread. She could live off those crumbs forever and never go hungry. She felt so lightheaded, she tripped over the foot of the beggar child. Ronaldo held on tightly, his flesh warming hers. Her strength increased by his.

"Don't forget," Brother Gregory said, "you lead the singing at sexte."

Ronaldo smiled. "I'm never late for the offices."

Brother Gregory shook his head. "That is true. But only because the conscience of an old man pricks you to duty." He found Ronaldo's hair and tousled it. "What will become of you when I am gone?"

Ronaldo set his basket in Brother Gregory's arms, steered him inside, and pushed the door shut behind him. "Come now," he said to Dell.

She walked beside him in a stupor. Here she was, making her way along a crowded street, breathing in the same foul air as yesterday, stepping through the same muck and dead animal parts. But somehow, with Ronaldo's arm linked in hers, the streets didn't seem as filthy or confusing as they had the day before.

They walked past the church with the shattered windows. That's how her life seemed—a thousand shards that needed to be put together into a single design. And she would do it—maybe not all at once, but slowly, piece by piece.

"Are you all right, then?" Ronaldo asked. "A bit steadier now?"

Was she? She nodded. Mayhap her mother and father had walked down this very street, laughing and holding hands. And now here *she* was, walking with the boy *she* loved. And all she could do was wag her head up and down like a donkey.

"Brother Gregory has never sent me off with a girl, you know. Nor allowed me to touch one."

Dell nodded again.

"I'm an almoner. I pass out food to the poor." He held her firmly, but he didn't squeeze or pinch. The place on her arm where his hand rested felt radiantly warm. She walked slowly, taking small steps, partly because she was weak and partly because she wanted to go on walking with Ronaldo forever.

"Take lemons, for instance," he said.

"Lemons?" Had he been talking about lemons? Startled, Dell turned and looked right into his eyes. Oh, his eyes! They were large and brown and so deep, she feared she might fall into them and drown.

"Others regard lemons as rare jewels. But not I. They're hard and bruised by the time Tomás brings them from across the sea."

"Tomás?"

"My brother, the merchant. He thinks an offering of

lemons twice a year is sufficient penance. I suppose they do serve a godly purpose—Brother Gregory gives them to the poor to sell."

Dell wanted to ask *which sea?* and *what penance?* but her lips wouldn't move.

"Brother Gregory tells me I must forgive my brother or my heart will grow sour and hard like the lemon."

Dell thought of *her* brother. Even though he exasperated her, she'd never been able to stay angry with him for long.

"My family was starving. So when Tomás came to England to seek his fortune, my parents sent me along. But Tomás was so much older, and I was nothing but a burden, an impediment. He left me at the gate, and Brother Gregory found me, whimpering like a baby." His fingers pressed into her arm. "And Tomás—he has grown into a man who is forthright and daring while I—I—"

"You have chosen a higher path."

He scowled. "I have been loyal and obedient, but I have *chosen* nothing."

She glanced sideways at him. Why was he revealing all these private thoughts to her? They didn't even know each other.

But maybe, in some mysterious way, they did. She felt as if she'd known him all her life. Her cheeks were hot. Was it possible that he felt the same way about her?

CHAPTER

XIX

Dell and Ronaldo continued on toward Dowgate Street, stopping to buy parsley and a thick slice of cheese. Maybe she *was* a temptress, an Eve. Every glance, every word that she and Ronaldo shared made her want him all the more.

Ahead of them a bull bellowed. "I am close to home now," she said. "Thank you for your kindness." She turned and sauntered away—trying to make her hips sway like Margery's.

"Wait," he called, and hurried after her. "Brother Gregory said I was to take you all the way to John the Joiner's. And look—I can see his sign from here."

"Is John your friend? When I was ill, I overheard you speaking to him down in the shop."

Ronaldo coughed. "Upon occasion ... I deliver things to him."

"Like you deliver things to my family on the mountain ... that is ... the *hill*? When the moon wanes again, my brother will be waiting for you by my mother's cross."

"I fear he'll be disappointed. These last weeks—Brother Gregory and I have been occupied with other matters."

"But that's impossible. You always come up the mountain."

Ronaldo steered her around a pile of fresh dung. "I'm sorry. I can tell you nothing more."

"Halloo?" Dell called, as she opened the door to the shop. "Halloo?" It didn't seem proper—to be in an empty house with a boy. But Ronaldo stepped inside, and Bartholomew, on his stick, smiled at them.

Ronaldo breathed deeply. "The scent of fresh-cut wood is a joy after. ..." He grinned and nodded in the direction of Butcher's Row.

Dell smiled back. How good it felt to have a real person with whom she could share a smile.

Ronaldo set down the bunch of parsley and picked up a hammer from the work bench. "I should like to be a carpenter—were I not to become a priest."

"My mother," Dell blurted out. "Lucretia. Do you know anything more about her?"

Ronaldo raised the hammer over his head and brought it down, with mock force, on a pine board. "After they escaped the palace, your family was poor. Brother Gregory gave your mother lemons to sell in the square. To supplement their meager wages."

"Did you ever see her—my mother?"

"Your cheeks are pale. Mayhap I should leave you now, so you can rest."

Dell shook her head and sat down at the work table. "Please. Sit down."

Ronaldo sat opposite her on a stool. "I hardly know where to begin." He brushed a mound of sawdust off the table, clearing a little spot where he laid his hands. "When my brother, Tomás, brought me to the monastery, I was a child of eight. I clung to him and begged him not to leave me.

"Brother Gregory was kind to me, but the food tasted strange, and the language sounded even stranger. I longed for home, for my mother. I grew thin and weak.

"Brother Gregory carried me to the square in hope of reviving me. Nothing worked. Not the acrobats, not the Gypsy dancers, not even the singing dog.

"And then—out of a bright blue booth—up popped a funny puppet dressed in a suit of brightly colored squares. I wouldn't budge until the puppet—and its puppeteer—came out of the booth to greet me."

"And that puppeteer was my mother?" Dell said.

Ronaldo nodded.

"But why is it that you have memories of her and I have none?" Heat rose in her cheeks. "It seems ... unfair."

"You were only four years old when she died. You were almost crushed under the booth with her, you know."

No, she didn't know. Or did she?

Ronaldo averted his eyes. "Maybe the shock of it shattered your memory."

"Sometimes fragments of things come to me."

"Anyway, after that first visit, Brother Gregory and I came daily. Lucretia always treated me as her own son. She even gave me honey and lemon to suck from her finger—just as she did for you and Nathaniel."

Dell startled. Honey and lemon. Her memory was true then. Perhaps her recurring dream was true also. "Did my father juggle lemons?" she ventured.

"He was a master. Why, he could keep five spinning at once."

All these pieces of her life—they'd been there all along. She just hadn't known what they meant or how to assemble them into a whole.

"That day—after the soldier rose up on his horse. ..." A shudder passed through Ronaldo's body. "I've never shown this to anyone." He rolled up the loose sleeve of his habit. "I wanted something to remember her by."

Dell drew in her breath. There, sewn inside his sleeve, was a strip of harlequin fabric—exactly like the piece that lay in Auntie's Bible. Dell reached out and drew her finger over the colored squares. *Velvet, satin, silk.* "My father owns a piece of this fabric also. But he never explained what it was." She leapt up, ran to get Bartholomew, and carried him back to the table. He lay on his back, smiling up at them. "My mother's puppet—did he look like this one?"

Ronaldo fingered the hem of Bartholomew's costume. "His very double. Even the harlequin pattern of his suit is the same. Except—no offense to your friend here—but this gentleman's costume is not as fine as the one your mother sewed."

"Bartholomew's is of cast-off scraps. It was all I had."

Dell leaned forward. "I have one more question. You told John that you had seen me on the mountain. Is that true?"

With one finger Ronaldo made a winding path through the sawdust toward Dell's fingers. "Yes, I saw you. Many times."

His finger came closer and closer. A shiver coursed up Dell's spine. "But how ... I hid myself."

Ronaldo traced around her fingers, almost touching them. "You're a terrible hider. Even as a child you were." He smiled. "The roots of the fir tree are so loosely woven, I could see right through them."

Flushing with embarrassment, Dell stared at her fingers—the ones Ronaldo had almost touched. "It's wrong for us to be here alone like this."

"Alone? What of this little man on the table?" Ronaldo withdrew his hands. "But mayhap you are right." He rose, bid her good morrow, and strode out the door.

"Wait," she cried out. "You forgot the parsley." She ran out to the street, but he was gone.

She carried Bartholomew, along with the bread and cheese, into the kitchen, and set the packages on the table. In one afternoon she'd learned more about her past than she had in twelve years on the mountain—the *hill*. Of all the discoveries she'd made, the one that mattered most to her was that her mother had loved her.

The hearth was cold and she shivered. A moment ago

Ronaldo's presence had kept her warm. But now the noises from the street blurred into an ugly din and the chill of the kitchen made her feel empty and alone.

She slipped Bartholomew on her hand. "I can never have Ronaldo," she said to him, "but at least I still have you."

"A great thanks for your loyalty, but even I know that a puppet is no fair exchange for the Boy." He pushed back his shoulders. "On the other hand, I'm not ashamed of who I am. On the contrary. I'm proud to be Bartholomew."

"Yes, you're a fine one. But what of me—am I Dell or Odelia?"

"Oh, pish. You are both Dell *and* Odelia—which makes you twice what you were yesterday."

Dell's stomach growled.

"And which makes you twice as hungry."

She set him back on his pine stick. She *was* hungry. Although the packages of bread and cheese lay before her, she didn't feel right taking food she hadn't earned.

Her mouth watered.

In the dim light of the kitchen, Ronaldo's face began to take form. His warm, brown skin, his bright eyes, his mischievous smile. Was her hunger making her see things? The vision melted, but the Boy would not go away. He pained her like a sharp stone in her shoe.

If she scrubbed the hearth and swept out the cinders, she could earn her supper. She heaved the iron cauldron off its hook and dragged it out into the room. There. Now she could clean every nook and cranny.

After she'd swept the cinders off the floor of the hearth, she brushed off the back wall. The gray ashes puffed up into a cloud, making her sneeze. She swept down the right wall and then the left. Strange—this left wall was cleaner than the other two. It looked newer but carelessly laid. Her broom struck a protruding brick and it fell into the cinders. A cloud of ash rose up.

Coughing, she pushed at another brick, and it wiggled like a loose tooth. "It's not firm," she called over her shoulder to Bartholomew. She shifted it back and forth, and it made a scraping sound as she wriggled it toward her. In a moment she held the cold brick in her hands. "This is most peculiar." She ought to replace it—this was none of her business. But hadn't she been patient and unquestioning long enough? John's father, for instance. Did he even exist? And all this talk of allegiance and treason. All these secrets.

She felt the next brick. It was as loose as the first, so she removed it as well. One brick after another came out, and she piled them up in the hearth, all the while listening for John's footsteps.

In a few moments she was staring at a dark opening big enough to crawl through. A smell like rotting mushrooms drifted out of it. Mayhap this was a sepulcher, where John buried his dead. The skin on her neck prickled.

Or maybe this den had something to do with John's unexplained comings and goings. She put one of the bricks back in place, then took it out again. "Bartholomew," she said, "what should I do?" When he made no reply, she hovered at the opening, put one hand through, and set it down on the chilly dirt floor. She put her other hand inside, then her right knee, and then her left. Her chest tightened.

Except for her feet, she was all the way inside now, and she could hardly breathe for fear and for the closeness of the space. It was quiet. Too quiet. Not a single vermin eye glowed at her. She moved her fingers over the dirt floor, listening.

The longer she knelt there, the smaller the space seemed to grow and the harder it became to breathe. She tried to right herself, but her head bumped a dirt ceiling. This place wasn't much bigger than the den of a fox.

She reached out one finger a little farther and it touched something. She recoiled, her heart thumping. She reached out again. A jug. She traced her fingers over its lip and sniffed. There was ale inside. Why would John keep a jug of ale. ...

The door of the shop slammed and Dell bolted upright, cracking her head on a brick. Flecks of light sparkled before her eyes but she scrambled backward, out of the tomb. Her hands shook as she shoved brick after brick back in place. From the shop came the cheerful sound of John's humming. Just one more row. There.

She rose and brushed the soot from her skirt. Bartholomew cast a questioning gaze over the cold hearth.

So many puzzles. All the talk of allegiance to the king and not the Pope. The ransacked churches. John's mysterious father and this secret den. And the word *treason* settling over everything like the cloud of ash. She'd had enough of silence and secrets. "I will make sense of these things," she whispered to Bartholomew. "See if I don't."

CHAPTER

XX

For over a fortnight, ever since May Day, John had used his spare moments to work on Dell's puppet booth. This morning he was fashioning a joint, and Dell was using a special adz to carve a hook on which to hang the curtain rod. She had hoped John would talk to her about his father, or about the secret space behind the hearth.

But John said nothing, concentrating all his efforts on a dovetail joint. What was she doing here, anyway? Although she'd been hired to read to John's father, the man was nowhere in sight. Dell had made herself useful in other ways—tidying the shop, cooking the pottage, mending John's jerkin. And John had been kind and generous to her. But still, something seemed amiss, and the time had come for straightforward speech.

"John," she said, trying to sound matter-of-fact. "When I was cleaning the hearth, I. ..."

A deafening *boom* exploded outside. The boards on the workbench jumped, and Bartholomew jiggled on his stick.

Dell dropped her tool and grabbed the edge of the workbench. *Boom!* The shutters rattled. *Merciful God,* she prayed, *Spare me, and I will never think on Ronaldo again.* She shut her eyes and covered her ears. When at last the explosions ended, she felt a gentle tug on her sleeve. John was sitting beside her. "Come now," he said. "The cannons are finished firing. The tyrant's foul deed is done."

Dell glanced around the room, uncertain why she was still alive and Bartholomew was still on his perch. "What tyrant?"

John rose to his feet. "You don't know then? No, of course you don't. Why would you?" He looked over his shoulder toward the door. "The guns were fired to proclaim the death of the queen." He leaned over the workbench and lowered his voice to a fierce whisper. "Today King Henry VIII cut off the head of his wife, Anne Boleyn."

"Anne Boleyn?" Hadn't that woman at the bakery called Anne Boleyn an adulterous whore? "I don't understand."

"Anne Boleyn gave him only one living daughter. Henry wants a male heir—not a frail thing in petticoats."

Dell shrank lower on the bench. Father had been right about this city. "Do other men in this city kill their wives for such an offense?"

"God's wounds!" John exclaimed. "We are not all brutes. But if the king wants something, he will have his way. And he will crush any who cross him."

Dell thought of her mother, Lucretia. She had been crushed, too—by one of the king's horses. "If King Henry desired a certain woman, but she escaped the palace with another man—might the king seek revenge on them?"

"If it fancied him to do so." John scratched his head. "Many a man has hanged just for poaching rabbits in the king's forest."

Bartholomew looked at her smugly. *I told you it was no accident,* he seemed to say. *I told you so.*

John shrugged. Then he fitted the two parts of the joint together. "Perfect! Has any approached you to sign the Oath of Allegiance?"

Dell straightened her back. "You asked me that once before. I have signed nothing."

"And are you willing to be of service to your God?"

"We must always serve God. But might we finish the puppet stage as well? It is I, not only Bartholomew, who desires it."

A knock on the door interrupted their conversation. A sharp rap, followed by two gentler ones. John hurried across the room and unbolted the door.

There stood Ronaldo, his face deep inside his black cowl. John closed and latched the door, and Ronaldo pushed back his hood. His breath was coming fast and hard.

"The king's men," he began. "Cromwell. ..." His gaze darted about the room. "I eluded them this time but ... they're closing in. ... Brother Gregory will never sign the Oath. ... we must act with haste." He stopped when he saw Dell, poised on the edge of the bench.

John motioned to her. "Come," he said in a quiet voice. He removed several coins from his purse and pressed them into her hand. "Go buy that fabric you fancied— for the curtain."

Dell glared at him and then at Ronaldo—at their tight lips and averted eyes. Only Bartholomew's gaze was clear, and it was riveted on the stage.

Dell clutched the coins in her fist. "No," she said, her voice defiant. "I won't leave. Not if Brother Gregory is in danger. You take me for an ignorant girl, but I know more than you think. I found that secret den in the hearth."

John's chin jerked up.

"And not only that," she said. "I don't want your charity." She hurled the coins at John and they bounced off his apron onto the floor. "I'm not a beggar. I came here to do useful work—to read to your blind father. Where is he? Answer me. What of him?"

Ronaldo shook his head. "I fear you need ask the worms *that* question."

"The worms?" Dell took a step toward John. "Your father is *dead*? Dead and buried?" How stupid she'd been not to have guessed it. "Why did you lie to me?"

John leaned over and picked a coin out of the sawdust. "All the lies I told you were in the interest of truth."

Ronaldo raised his eyebrows. "Lying for truth, John? You know what Brother Gregory would say about that."

John sat down and laid his cap beside him. "All right, then." He ran his fingers through his strawlike hair and spoke to the table. "It is I—not my dead father—who wants reading to. And not reading only, but writing as well. I need someone to write letters for me. Letters of a private and delicate nature."

"But *you're* not blind," Dell sputtered. "Why don't you do it yourself?"

John blushed. "I received but little schooling. And the job requires more than reading and writing. We need a person who can walk the streets unnoticed by Cromwell and his henchmen. Someone who can deliver letters to certain monasteries."

"John," Ronaldo said. "You must not draw her into this. The king's men are everywhere. And she has suffered enough."

Dell pushed back her shoulders. The king had taken her mother's life, and now it appeared that he wanted Brother Gregory's as well. "What if I *want* to be drawn into it?"

"If that is what you truly choose," John said, "then you must be able to find your way to the Benedictine monastery."

Ronaldo turned to Dell. "I beg of you. Don't do what John asks. You will be putting yourself in grave danger."

"I will do it." Dell crossed her arms over her chest. She would find out later exactly what the danger was, just as she would solve the mystery of the secret den. But for now she wanted John and Ronaldo to know that she was not a girl to be trifled with. She would be a part of this ... this endeavor ... whatever it was.

Dell glanced at Bartholomew. His eyes burned with accusations: *Will you abandon me now? What of my dreams? What of our future together?*

CHAPTER

XXI

Dell walked along Thames Street at a moderate pace, carrying the basket over one arm. She swallowed the lump in her throat and tried not to think about the letter she'd written or the secret place in the hearth. For the last week she'd been doing exactly what she wanted to be doing— returning to the monastery where she might see Ronaldo and ask Brother Gregory more questions about her mother. She held the basket close to her side, but not too close, in hopes of looking like an ordinary girl on her way home from marketing.

John had filled the basket with aging onions and turnips from his larder and covered the pile of vegetables with a square of linen cloth. No one had spoken of the letter that lay—still as a dead fish—on the bottom of the basket.

John remained tight-lipped about the meaning of his letters, but Dell had her suspicions about them. This letter was a queer one, talking about wolves who prowled— even now—around the fold, hungry for innocent sheep. It talked about leading the sheep through Aldersgate at the next slender moon. That last part was nonsense—even Dell knew that—the city gates all closed at curfew. *Make haste,* the letter concluded, *the time is ripe for slaughter.*

She walked with her head down, lost in thought, and didn't notice until it was too late that she had walked directly into Margery's bosom. Several onions toppled from the basket, and Dell hurriedly picked them up and tucked them back under the cloth. If only she'd turned earlier, onto Knightrider Street.

Margery's eyes were full of fire. With one finger she poked at Dell's chest. "So," she said, prodding Dell so hard, she stumbled back a step. "How many times do you be doing the act with him?"

Dell clutched at her bodice. She could tell from Margery's fury that the *him* was Ronaldo, but the *act*? She let out a gasp. "Surely you don't think—"

"I don't gots to think. I sees the lust in your eyes."

"I've only just touched him."

"Oh, I believe you—that be certain—but where? That's what I be wanting to know. And with what?" She leaned close to Dell and gave her teat a sharp tweak.

Dell's hand flew at Margery's face. The sharp *slapping* sound shocked Dell. She looked at her tingling hand and then at the red blotch that spread across Margery's pale skin.

Margery had barely flinched. "I sees you got some sauce after all."

Dell pushed her hair behind her ears and pulled herself up straight. "I would never steal a man from the church. It's a sin against God."

"I don't be worrying much about God. He be getting

whatever he wants. But me, I be a fishmonger's daughter, and I gots to fight for what I wants. And so do you."

"That's blasphemy."

"It be the truth, and you knows it."

Margery was right. Even though Dell was fighting against her feelings for Ronaldo, she was losing the battle. She could smell—even now—the sharp spicy scent of his body. And she could feel the spot on her arm where his fingers had wreathed it. She *did* want him. She wanted Ronaldo just as much as—no—more than Margery. "There's no use fighting God," she said. "He will always win."

"Well, before he does, we best be enjoying ourselves." Margery set her hands on her hips. "If my da be getting *his* way, he be marrying me off to the tanner." She squeezed her nose shut with her finger and thumb. "I shall need cover my face with a cloth soaked in vinegar to lay me down in *his* marriage bed." She whisked the linen square off Dell's basket and draped it over her head and face to demonstrate. "Or maybe I shall wear this—like a veil— and go to Ronaldo." She blew on the cloth and it fluttered in front of her. "Behold," I be saying to him. "I be a angel of God bringing you great joy before you renounce your fleshly ways." She rotated her hips, grinding them against Dell's.

Dell snatched the linen square off Margery's head. Not only was Margery blaspheming God, but she had also removed a covering of secrecy from the basket. Without the cloth, the letter was one layer closer to the light.

But even worse, Margery had said—right out loud—the thoughts that burned in her own mind—thoughts about how Ronaldo would kiss her brow and then her cheek and then her lips and then—she didn't know what else.

"Well, you may be innocent, and you may be a sly whore, but one thing be plain. I gots what God—and you—aren't got." With that, she cupped one of her bosoms in each hand and pushed them nearly up to her neck. "And I gots more somewhere else."

While Dell stood speechless, Margery dropped her arms, sidled close, and grabbed Dell in the pissing place. Dell gave her a shove.

Margery laughed. "You be jealous, Mistress Sour, and don't be denying it. You be nothing but meager in all your parts. Why, even your name be measly."

"My name is Odelia."

"Ah—a great pardon then, *Lady Odelia*." Margery bowed her head close to Dell's basket. She wrinkled her nose. "Who be selling you *those* turnips?" She poked at one. "Why, these be hardly fit for the pigs."

Dell arranged the cloth over the vegetables. "I'm not buying," she said. "I—I'm delivering."

"Do that be so?" Margery said. "And what pigs do you be delivering to?"

Dell put her hand in front of her mouth to muffle her answer. "The Benedictine ones."

"The *what*?" Margery said. "You must be speaking up loud if you hopes to get a man. If you hopes to get anything."

She put her arm through Dell's and dragged her forward. "I mights as well come along with you as sell my oysters alone. You be a odd one—make no mistake—but not so queer as you those two fortnights ago."

"Are you certain you want to come along?" What a foolish question. Margery was not a questioner, like Dell. No matter how many times Margery changed her opinions, she was always certain of every one.

"Do you know what I needs most?" Margery began. She pulled Dell close. "What I needs most is a velvet ribbon— a red one—to tie around my neck so I looks like a fine lady—because then a rich merchant be begging my hand." Margery raised her hand delicately into the air, offering it to the imaginary suitor. "And also a ball of lavender soap to be washing away the smell of fish. Those two things— that's what I be needing most."

The thought of Margery marrying a rich merchant both heartened and confused Dell. "What about Ronaldo? Don't you love *him*?"

"Love? Do you imagine a fishmonger's daughter gots time for love? Only kings and queens gots time for l-o-o-o-o-v-e." She drew out the last word as if it were a long red velvet ribbon binding two lovers' hearts together forever.

"But what about King Henry? *He* had time to love his wife, and he cut off her head."

Margery gave Dell a sharp stab with her elbow. "Do you be speaking ill of our good king? He needs an heir, does he not?"

Dell winced at the pang in her side. "No. I'm only saying the truth. Didn't you hear the cannons?"

Margery spoke into Dell's ear. "Anne Boleyn was a witch." Margery wriggled her fingers in Dell's face. "I be hearing she had six of these. *Six*. She be deserving what she got." Margery's voice shrank to a whisper. "She be doing the act with her own brother. And she be a traitor."

Dell's skin crawled. John had not called Henry a good king. John had called him a tyrant, but only in a whispered voice. She thought about the words on the handbill. *The king, not the Pope, is the supreme head of the Church of England. Any seditious writing or talk shall be considered treason against the crown.* If a monk were to speak out for the Pope, would those words be considered seditious? Would that monk be a traitor?

A wave of fear washed over her. Of course John's letter wasn't about real sheep and real wolves. Why would he conceal a letter about livestock? No, his messages to Brother Gregory were written in a kind of code. Some of the messages puzzled her, but she understood enough. She pulled the basket close to her breast.

All around her, people pushed and shouted and cajoled just as they had done yesterday and the day before that. But now something had changed. *She* had changed. She was no longer an ignorant outsider. She was a part of something. But belonging, she realized now, had its own dilemmas. For instance, what of Bartholomew? Would her decision to work for John destroy her dream of being Bartholomew's puppeteer? By the time she and Margery arrived at the monastery gates, Dell's armpits were soaked with sweat.

Margery glared at the door and then at Dell. "Pigs indeed," she said with a huff. "You do be a sly one, don't you? Sneaking here to see your sweetheart."

Dell didn't answer. It would be safer if Margery believed that Dell had come simply to tease Ronaldo. She knocked on the door, and then she knocked again. She would not give up until someone slid the lock.

Margery tugged at her curls and pinched her cheeks until they turned pink. "The point be that now I gets to see his pretty face, too. Ho, there!" she shouted. "Ho, inside there!" She banged on the door with her fist. "He knows you be coming, don't he?"

"No," Dell said. "I told you. I've come to deliver this basket to Brother Gregory."

Margery pounded on the door again. "You," she said, "be the most deceivingest strumpet this side of the Thames."

Just behind them, a horse whinnied.

Margery turned and clutched her breast. "Oh, my heart," she choked.

CHAPTER

XXII

Dell followed Margery's wide-eyed gaze. A young man wearing a velvet cape leapt from a cart laden with wooden crates. He tossed a farthing at the twisted beggar girl. Margery's gaze followed the man as he paced alongside the gate.

The man spun on his heel and marched the other way, rubbing his hands together. He seemed so impatient, Dell stepped out of his way. Margery stood, spellbound. The man yanked the paten that protected his shoe and slammed it against the door with such force, the beggar girl dropped the farthing.

The man muttered something in a language Dell didn't understand. A Latin prayer? No—the words were too loud and angry. Only one rang clear—*Ronaldo*. The man banged his paten on the door again.

Margery's hands fumbled at her bare throat. At last the huge door creaked open.

"Welcome, my son," Brother Gregory said. "We knew it was you by the sound of your knocking."

"Good morrow," said the man.

Ronaldo stood beside Brother Gregory, staring down at his feet. "Good morrow, Tomás," he mumbled.

Tomás. Dell sucked in her breath. This was Ronaldo's

brother from across the sea. He had Ronaldo's brown hair and eyes. His skin was brown, too, but not as dark as his younger brother's. Tomás was taller, and his nose was a commanding one, not crooked like Ronaldo's. Only Tomás's impatience made him seem unrelated to Ronaldo.

Tomás pointed at the cart. "I've brought you blankets. And lemons. An entire crate of them."

Dell stared at the open crate. It was piled to the top with the bright yellow fruits.

"As you know," said Brother Gregory, "God provides us monks with all that we need." He nodded at the row of beggars that lined the monastery wall. "Ronaldo, pass out the lemons to our less fortunate brothers and sisters."

"But they're too valuable to—" Tomás sputtered.

"Indeed. Each one will draw a precious penny or two in the market." Brother Gregory fumbled about until his hand touched Dell's shoulder. "Do you remember, Odelia, how selling Tomás's lemons kept your family from starvation?"

"I remember how they tasted and smelled."

Margery gave a little cough and tucked her curls into her cap.

Dell hugged her basket close. With every passing moment it grew heavier and heavier. She had hoped she would see Ronaldo today, but not like this—not in the presence of Margery and Tomás. And what if Margery asked more questions about the rotting vegetables? Dell pressed her back against the wall, hoping to become as invisible as a beggar. Ronaldo continued to stare at his feet.

Tomás looked him up and down. "You are well, then?"

Ronaldo nodded.

"And you remain a loyal and obedient subject of the king?"

Brother Gregory answered. "A monk is, above all, a loyal and obedient subject to God, our highest authority, and to the Pope, who is ordained by God to lead His people." The aged man's words were so much firmer than his frail body. "Surely the monks in your country live by the same vows as our brothers here."

"I have heard the news, Brother. The three Carthusian monks who remained loyal to the Pope were hanged at Tyburn. Before they died, they were drawn and quartered. If you do not value your own life, consider the peril to my brother."

Brother Gregory didn't answer. His milky eyes drifted upward.

What vile monster would cut open a living monk and rip out his bowels? Dell thought of Father's words. *You know why it is called the City of Cannibals. It is because men eat each other's flesh, drink each other's blood.* Her brow broke out in a sweat. Sheep and wolves. She twisted the linen cloth until it was a damp wad in her fist.

Running errands in secret was frightening enough. But Brother Gregory was professing loyalty to the Pope in public. His words would be deemed treason. Where did he find such courage? Margery stood close by, casting sideways glances at the cart laden with gifts.

Ronaldo continued to stare at his feet. "How is Father?"

Tomás laughed. "Plagued by a rotten tooth. He howls to beat the devil, but allows no man to pull it."

Ronaldo's lips turned up. "And Mamá?"

"She promises to light a special candle for you in July, on the Feast Day of St. James."

Ronaldo's smile vanished. "The day of my final vows— less than eight weeks hence. Give her my thanks."

Eight weeks. Dell's gut felt heavy, as if she had just swallowed—whole—one of the onions in her basket. Margery seemed overcome as well, and she broke into a loud bout of coughing.

"Tomás," said Brother Gregory, "whose womanly voice do I hear? Have you taken a wife?"

At the word *wife*, Margery's coughing turned into a violent attack of hiccups. Dell patted her on the back, and Tomás withdrew an embroidered cloth from his jerkin and offered it to her.

Dell laid a hand on Brother Gregory's arm. "It is I," she said. "Odelia. The one coughing is my friend, Margery." Margery made a little curtsey to Brother Gregory and then a deeper one to Tomás. When she leaned over in front of him, her bosoms squeezed out the top of her bodice and pulsed with every cough.

"I've brought something for you," Dell went on, trying to keep her voice even. "A basket of vegetables from John the Joiner."

For the first time, Ronaldo raised his eyes. He looked

at Dell and then the basket, but his expression remained blank.

"Ah, John the Joiner," said Brother Gregory. "Another generous benefactor." He nudged Ronaldo, and the boy stepped forward and removed the basket from Dell's arm. His fingers brushed her hand, and a pleasant shiver ran the length of her spine.

"You appear much pleased to receive a pile of rotting vegetables." Tomás nodded toward his cart. "Perhaps one of you could show the same eagerness in helping me unload *my* gifts."

"I be eager," Margery said.

Tomás smiled. "A woman who embraces hard work," he said. He turned to Ronaldo. "Mamá would like that."

"I wouldn't know," Ronaldo mumbled. He gave the basket to Brother Gregory, carefully sliding it along the old man's arm, nearly all the way to his elbow. Then Ronaldo and Margery and Dell helped Tomás carry the crates inside the monastery walls.

Dell shivered. Brother Gregory—a traitor. She felt sick and cold, as if the whole world had just turned to winter. Margery, on the other hand, seemed to glow with the flush of spring. Her eyes darted back and forth between Tomás and Ronaldo, like two humblebees uncertain of the sweetest flower.

Tomás leaned toward her. "Have you a fever?" he asked.

Margery laid the back of her hand on her brow. "No,"

she said. "That is—yes—I believe I do. I believe I be about to faint."

Tomás nodded at his cart. "Might I offer you a ride home? My brother will attest that I am an honorable man." When Margery responded with another fit of coughing, he added, "You haven't contracted the pestilence, have you?"

"Oh, no. It be only my delicate nature."

Tomás sniffed the air. "New Fish Street, then?"

Margery beamed. "How do you be knowing?"

Tomás didn't reply, but assisted her into the cart.

"Good riddance," Ronaldo mumbled.

Brother Gregory hunched over again, causing the hump under his shoulders to stand out in greater prominence. "Be thankful for your brother's visit. God despises an ungrateful heart."

Ronaldo clenched and unclenched his fist. "Yes, Brother."

"And for your mother, who prays for you."

"*My* mother sent me away." Ronaldo's voice was sharp. "Lucretia was mother to me."

Brother Gregory laid a hand on Ronaldo's shoulder. "You must soften your heart, my son. Your mother believed you would have a better life here in England."

Brother Gregory held fast to the basket. "Wait here—both of you. I will return shortly." He turned and walked into the stack of boxes. His shin bone cracked against a sharp corner of wood, and he let out a little grunt of pain. Several turnips tumbled out of the basket and rolled—

thankfully—out of his way. He shuffled along a path that led to a stone building behind a neatly trimmed hedgerow.

Ronaldo closed the door behind Brother Gregory and pressed his brow against it.

Dell understood what it felt like to lose a mother. And Ronaldo had lost not only his own Mamá, but Lucretia as well. And now Brother Gregory was in peril. She longed to lay a hand on Ronaldo's shoulder, to tell him she understood. But touching him would be a sign that she was lustful and desirous of him.

She took a step forward. She wanted to move her fingers down the sloping line of his nose, over the place where the bone jutted out at a crooked angle under his smooth skin. She wanted to trace the outline of his jaw, the stipple of his beard. Would touching this boy, who was almost a monk, make her a whore?

She reached out her hand, then withdrew it. No. It would be a grievous sin to touch him. Ronaldo belonged to God, not to her.

CHAPTER

XXIII

All right, then. If Dell couldn't touch Ronaldo, at least she could ask him for information that would allay her suspicions. She waited until he turned from the door, then drew herself up tall. "You must speak openly with me about Brother Gregory and the danger he is in."

"I've told you. I cannot." His cheeks paled suddenly and he grabbed the blanket off the beggar girl. "Sit," he hissed. He shoved Dell to the ground and threw the blanket at her. "Hide yourself."

She fell hands first and a little jolt of pain shot up one arm. Stunned, she huddled next to the beggar and pulled the blanket over her head. Hoof beats clattered close by, louder and louder. Ronaldo laid his hand on her shoulder and intoned a Latin prayer.

Dell peered out through a narrow opening in the folds of the blanket. The horse's huge hoof stopped barely an arm's length away, and she drew back in alarm. The shaggy hoof was grimed from the muck of the street and was big as a round of bread.

"Good morrow, Lord Cromwell," Ronaldo said.

Cromwell—the man Ronaldo had spoken about with such fear and urgency at John's.

A deep voice came from above the horse. "Where is the old monk—your teacher?" The hoof stomped on the dirt. "You are his eyes and his crutch, so he cannot be far."

"He is at prayer," Ronaldo answered. "He cannot be disturbed."

Cromwell laughed. "Well, when the old man is done with his praying, remind him that he owes allegiance to the Crown, not the Pope. Remind him that His Majesty's demands are simple: every knee must bend and every head must bow." The horse snorted. "Every one."

"Sir," Ronaldo said, "every day Brother Gregory kneels and bows his head in prayer. He is a faithful servant of God."

The man's voice seemed to come closer. "And what of *you*, Ronaldo?"

Dell sucked in her breath. This man knew Ronaldo's name and spoke it slowly, stretching it into something twisted and distorted.

"And what of you?" Cromwell repeated, his voice cold with disdain. "Are you also *a servant of God?* Or should I say *a puppet of the Pope?*"

The hem of Ronaldo's habit quivered, but his feet remained firmly planted. "We must render unto Caesar the things that are Caesar's and unto God the things that are God's."

"Brother Gregory has taught you well. Mayhap I shall mark your words in my book of names. That way, we will not forget your pious sentiments, and I can convey them to the king. Good day."

"They are not my sentiments, sir. They are the words of Christ."

The man tossed a farthing at Dell's feet. The beggar girl lunged for it, but her rigid body fell against the leg of the horse. The creature shimmied in surprise, and a small black book toppled into the street, inches from Dell.

The book of names. Dell snatched it up. No! She would not let Cromwell write Ronaldo's name in it. The man leaned over the side of the horse, and Dell gasped. This was the same man who had followed the procession of monks to the monastery. His jowls hung loose and lazy, but his eyes burned like the eyes of a hungry wolf. The blanket fell from Dell's shoulders, leaving her uncovered except for the man's shadow.

His eyes all but disappeared in the folds of his flesh, and he spoke in an ugly whisper. "Haven't I seen you before?" He licked his thin lips. "Your name?"

"Dell, sir. Odelia."

He turned his gloved hand palm up and waited for Dell to lay the book on it. Then he straightened himself and jerked on the horse's reins. The creature turned and pranced away. Dell stared down at her feet. What had she done?

When she finally gathered the courage to look up again, Ronaldo's hand was outstretched. Dell grabbed it greedily, the way the beggar girl seized bread. Ronaldo's fingers, like hers, were trembling and so slick with sweat, she almost slipped from his grasp. But he held fast, and in a moment she was on her feet.

It seemed as if he needed the reassurance of her touch as much as she needed his. But that was a silly notion—he was a boy, almost a man—and men didn't yearn for such girlish things. Embarrassed, she pulled her hand away.

"Why did you pick up Cromwell's book?" he asked, his voice taut with anger. "What were his whisperings to you? I could not hear over the gurgling of the beggar girl."

"Nothing. He takes me for a beggar. That's all. Nothing more."

The monastery gate creaked open and Brother Gregory limped out. Thank Heaven he hadn't seen how stupidly she had grabbed Cromwell's book ... how hungrily she had grasped Ronaldo's hand.

Ronaldo pulled open the gate, and Brother Gregory shuffled forward, the basket on his arm and a smile on his lips.

"He was here again," Ronaldo said to him, "while you ... were at prayer."

Brother Gregory nodded. His lip twitched for just a moment, and then it eased back into its serene smile. How could he be so calm? His eyes drifted this way and that, like Noah's dove searching for a bit of dry land. They settled finally on Dell's face. "Odelia," he said. "Thank you for carrying this basket. You are like your mother—strong and good—a woman who resists evil."

Dell's cheeks burned. Strong—ha! Her hands still trembled from her encounter with Cromwell—the Wolf. And good? If Brother Gregory had seen how she grabbed at Ronaldo, he would not call her good. She shuddered. Where had strength and goodness gotten her mother? The grave, that's where. No, Dell did not want to die.

She wanted to build her puppet stage, so Bartholomew could become an actor and she a puppeteer. She wanted to smell Margery's fishy scent. She wanted to hold Ronaldo's hand. No, she was neither good nor strong. She wanted to be part of this stinking, living city.

Brother Gregory seemed to read her thoughts. "If any ask you to sign the Oath of Allegiance," he continued, "it would behoove you to do so. Else the king has the right to take your head."

"I will think on it." But how could she swear allegiance to a king who had murdered her mother? How could she promise loyalty to a king who was bent on murdering Brother Gregory and maybe Ronaldo? No, she could never do it.

Brother Gregory fumbled for her hand and took it in his. Could he tell that her fingers had touched Ronaldo's? But the monk merely patted her hand and slipped the basket onto her arm. Dell let out her breath and lifted a corner of the linen cloth. Turnips and onions. The same ones she'd brought to the monastery.

"Take this to John the Joiner," he said. "Do not linger. He's expecting the vegetables for his supper."

Dell swallowed the lump of fear in her throat. If she had kept the blanket over her head, Cromwell would not have noticed her. He would not know who she was.

"Odelia?" Brother Gregory said.

Dell startled at the sound of her name. Her hands shook, and her heart pounded loud enough for the whole city to hear. She scurried away, looking—she hoped—like a simple girl who had tarried too long with her sweetheart.

As she walked along Bread Street, the *clop-clop* of a horse sounded behind her. "It's nothing," she told herself. "The city is full of horses." She walked faster, but the hoof beats only grew louder. In a moment, the creature had caught up to her. Out of the corner of her eye, she could see the white flank, heaving with impatience.

Get away! she wanted to scream. *Leave me alone!* But instead she continued her steady pace, eyes down, clutching the basket to her bosom. At last, when she turned onto Butcher's Row, Cromwell spurred his horse in the opposite direction—away from the bellowing of the bulls and the stink of their slaughter.

So Cromwell's black book was a list of names. How important a name was! And now she had not one, but two. The girl named Dell she knew. But who was Odelia? And how might this new person act? Unlike Brother Gregory, Odelia wouldn't give her life for love of church. And unlike Ronaldo, Odelia wouldn't follow Brother Gregory to the scaffold out of loyalty. But King Henry had killed Lucretia—he had robbed Odelia of her mother. And neither Dell nor Odelia would bow to such a man as that.

XXIV

As the days of early June lengthened, Dell and John used the additional moments of light to complete the puppet booth. They spoke little, but John hummed while they worked. She wanted to believe that his lightheartedness was real, but he continued to dictate letters, and she continued to deliver them. Yesterday she'd brought Brother Gregory a bundle of clothing—a skirt and bodice and a blue apprentice suit. *Cast-offs for the poor,* John had told her. But what would John be doing with a cast-off skirt and bodice?

He had cut the front wall of the booth to a perfect size, so when Dell knelt behind it and raised her puppets, not a strand of her black hair showed. While he planed the wood, Dell sewed her curtain. She spread the blue fabric on the workbench and laid her cheek on it. It reminded her of those afternoons when the Boy had looked up at the wide expanse of sky on the mountain and grinned in delight. How long ago those days seemed!

In truth, her time in the city had been brief. Since she'd arrived, both the lean moon and her bleeding had come but once.

John insisted that every joint in the booth be perfectly

secure. Yesterday he had carved the protruding tenons—no bigger than his thumb—on both ends of the stage. Today he was chiseling out the matching grooves, or mortises, in the side walls. The tenons would fit snugly into the mortises, forming joints that would hold the stage in place. Last week he'd even surprised Dell with paints so she could make the booth bright and colorful for Whitsunday.

From his perch on the shelf, Bartholomew watched his stage take form, beaming in anticipation. How happy he would be when he could sing and dance in front of the whole world. He had watched as Dell made another puppet—a girl with yellow braids. Now she was working on a third puppet. So far it was only a hollowed-out squash and a bit of red fabric, but soon it would be the devil, complete with horns and a pointy tail.

Dell nodded at the girl puppet drying on the shelf. "So, Bartholomew. What do you think of your new helpmate?" When he refused to answer, she went on. "She'll be lovely, I promise you, and you must think of a proper name for her."

"I believe he's jealous," John said with a wry smile. "Look at his stony countenance."

"No, not jealous," she said. "He's remembering his old friend, Eleanor."

The light in the room began to fade. If she worked quickly, she might be able to finish the curtain before dusk. Her needle darted in and out of the fabric, but her thoughts were not so easily pinned down. Would Cromwell—the

Wolf—return to the monastery to carry out his threats? How soon?

Whitsunday dawned chilly with the faintest hint of sunlight—a perfect day for a celebration. By the time she came downstairs, John was at the hearth, poking about in the cold ashes. Outside, the Sabbath bells pealed.

"Have a care when you go out today," John said. He took Dell's shawl off the peg. "Cover your head and go to St. Paul's by way of Thames Street. I will take Knightrider Street, and we will stand apart from one another at Mass. Do not draw attention to yourself."

Dell took the shawl and hung it back up. "You go on," she said. "I want to practice my puppet play once more before the festivities."

He returned the shawl to her hands. "All citizens are required by law to attend."

What a queer law. Dell took the shawl and wrapped it around her head. Well, at least Mass at St. Paul's would be less painful than kneeling on sharp pebbles in Auntie's grotto.

The din at the back of the church was even louder than it had been the day she'd followed the procession of monks inside. A vendor trod on her toes and waved a fistful of ribbons in her face. Oh, how Margery would sigh after that slim crimson one! Just as Dell pulled away, something prodded her backside. A pickpocket! She swung around.

But the poking object wasn't a hand. It was a stick. And at the other end of it was the stump-legged beggar woman.

"A very pretty shawl," she whined, giving Dell an extra jab. "And a costly one, too." She cackled and lifted her skirt. "I would spread my legs for a penny, too, but you see how it is."

Taut with anger, Dell glared down at the woman and her hideous oozing stumps. "I am not like you," she said. "*I am earning an honest wage.*" Even as she spoke, her cruel words echoed off the sacred walls of the church and reverberated inside her head. And the frightening part was—she savored them. She enjoyed looking down on this repugnant woman and spewing spiteful words at her.

Then guilt panged her. Brother Gregory would have laid his hand on the woman's vermin-infested hair and blessed her. He would have said that we are all beggars in the sight of God.

And here Dell was—on the Sabbath of all days—seething with hatred for this pitiful woman. Dell averted her eyes from the stained glass angels and moved deeper into the church. John had told her not to draw attention to herself, to act like everyone else. If only she knew how.

A woman great with child shuffled forward. As she moved along, she made a series of shallow bows and mumbled, "God have mercy, Christ have mercy, God have mercy." Her hands were folded prayerfully on her huge belly and her eyes were fixed on the crucifix. Dell imitated her. She knelt when the woman knelt, crossed herself when the woman did, and moved her lips whenever the woman muttered whatever it was she was muttering.

Puffs of incense drifted to the vaulted heights of the church, and Dell's eyes watered. She tried to follow the chanting of the priest, but his Latin words, like the incense, were nothing but a thick haze.

She fixed her gaze on the silver crucifix that stood on the altar and tried to direct her thoughts to God. But the gray haze made her think of the soot-filled air of the hearth.

That secret den had something to do with wolves and sheep, with Brother Gregory and Cromwell. Was it a hiding place for John's correspondence with the monks? She didn't think the letters had mentioned a den, but often the messages were encrypted. She made the sign of the cross and prayed that God would preserve the lives of Ronaldo and Brother Gregory.

Suddenly the urge to piss struck her, and she squeezed her pissing muscles tight. She couldn't just walk out and she couldn't make water on the floor of the church. She crossed her legs. She'd been so excited about her puppet show this morning, she'd forgotten to use the chamber pot.

She prayed for John and Margery and for the health of Margery's little brother, Ned. She pressed her hand into her pissing place. She even prayed for Father and Auntie. She couldn't forgive them for their cruelties, but she understood why they had tried to prevent her from coming to the city. Last, she prayed for Nathaniel. Despite her brother's surliness, she missed him. Who would watch him juggle his pinecones now that she was gone?

The priest lifted the host off a silver plate. He held it up for all to see, then laid it on his tongue. Everyone—including Dell—knelt and made the sign of the cross and mumbled something. Then the priest held up a great silver chalice and drank from it. More crossing and some moaning, too. Dell helped the pregnant woman to her feet, relieved that her birthing pains hadn't started in church. Although if this Mass didn't end soon. ...

Hours later—or maybe it was days or weeks or years later—she wasn't sure—she rushed from the church, blinking in the daylight. At last! She dashed to the nearest alley, pulled down her leggings, and squatted. And squatted. Nothing in her life had ever felt this good. Except, of course, the warmth of Ronaldo's hand around hers. She ran the rest of the way home.

When she entered the shop, John was already there, a rope hanging over one arm. He wasn't even out of breath. "Let me secure the booth for you," he said.

"I ran the whole way," Dell said, still panting. "How did you arrive here before me?"

He looped the rope twice around the booth. His hands were black with soot. Something was amiss.

"John," she said, "have *you* signed the Oath of Allegiance?"

John cinched the knot tight. "It is not *my* signature the king requires. At least not yet."

"Then your name is not written in Cromwell's book?"

John gave a violent start. "No. Nor is yours, as long as you do your work quietly and without question." He formed the rope into a handle for carrying.

"But how do you expect me to be a part of—"

"Hold fast to your things," John said with a wink. "The thieves will be celebrating with the same excess as the honest folk."

She snatched up her sack of puppets. Why would he never be honest with her? "But *you'll* be there to keep watch."

John shook his head. "I can't accompany you," he said. "You understand."

"No, I don't," Dell said. She had presumed he would be in the front row, laughing and applauding even if no one else did. Why couldn't her show be something separate, untouched by worldly troubles? "Nevermind, then. I'll carry on without you."

She grabbed the carrying rope and dragged her stage toward the door. Pish on John and his secrets. For Bartholomew and her, today would be a day to celebrate their accomplishments. Still, her throat tightened, as if a noose had been cinched around it.

XXV

By the time she arrived, the square was already a riot of color and sounds and smells. And people. Colorful pennants—red and yellow and blue—fluttered to the melodies of lyres and lutes. A minstrel sang a ballad about Robin Hood and Maid Marian, and an ape on a rope tipped his hat at her. The air was so rich with the aromas of pasties and tarts and pies, Dell's belly felt satisfied just from breathing in the delicious scents.

The rope that secured the puppet booth had begun to cut into her hand so she was relieved when she found a spot to set up her stage. On her left was a Gypsy woman spreading out her cards on a rug, and on her right were two dwarves juggling sticks of fire. They wore matching green vests, and appeared to be father and son. The boy, who was younger than Dell, juggled with the same cheerful cockiness as Nathaniel. Did he know that Father had kept five lemons spinning at once? She felt a pang of missing her brother.

As she opened her sack of puppets, a group of men bedecked in tassels and ribbons skipped by her. She smiled. These must be the morris dancers John had told her about. Their hosen were covered with little bells that jingled as the men danced.

She held one wall of her booth upright, then leaned a second wall against the first. She bent over to pick up the third, when someone rubbed her backside. She whirled around. "How dare you!"

The someone was a horse. Not Cromwell's—thank Heaven—not even a real horse—but a man wearing a horse head and a horse costume. He tried to nuzzle Dell's backside again, but she gave him a shove. The two jugglers laughed, but the horse gave a pitiful whinny and pranced away.

She leaned the boards together again. Keeping all three walls upright at the same time was tricky. Before today John had steadied them while she fitted the joints.

The older juggler approached her. "We be willing to lend a hand," he said.

"Thank you," Dell said. "I would be most grateful."

When all three walls of the booth were secure and the stage and curtain were in place, Dell stepped inside. She slipped Bartholomew on her right hand and the new puppet, Daisy, on her left. "Ready?" she asked. They nodded. She peeked out around the side of the booth. Her insides twitched. "There's no audience," she said.

Bartholomew made a little growling sound in his throat. "That's because we've done nothing to attract one."

He was right. Dell stood inside the booth, her arms rigid as the beggar girl's. She had no idea how to draw a crowd. After all those hours of practicing, all those afternoons building and painting and sewing. Now what?

As the puppets stood motionless on the stage, something

tugged at Dell's skirt. She glanced down, ready to give the intruder a hearty kick. "Jennet!" Dell cried. "It's you!"

Margery's little sister stood there, one hand clutching Dell's skirt. She was sucking her thumb with great vigor and staring at Bartholomew. From the other side of the booth came Margery's frantic shouts.

"Jennet!" she cried. "Don't you be hiding from me, Jennet! You hear? Jennet—you come out right now! Naughty Jennet! Naughty, *naughty* Jennet!"

When Dell, a puppet on each hand, and Jennet emerged from the booth, Margery grabbed her little sister by the arm and shook her so hard, her thumb popped out of her mouth. "Shame on you, Jennet! Shame!"

Jennet, her eyes fixed on Bartholomew, put her thumb back in place and sucked harder than ever.

Margery's four brothers clustered around Dell, all of them staring, wide-eyed, at the puppets. Between Matthew and Mark stood Ned. He was here—alive and well. A little wave of happiness washed over Dell—her act of kindness had mattered. The boy was pale but as eager and wide-eyed as his brothers.

Margery gaped at Dell. "By my troth!" she cried. "It be you!" Her gaze darted from Dell to Bartholomew to Daisy and back to Dell again. "You be telling me this—the very first day—that you be a puppet master. And here you be, by Heaven, here you be!" She looked back over her shoulder, and her expression sobered. "But nobody be watching you. Excepting these two." She tipped her head in the direction of the two jugglers, who had interrupted their own performance in order to watch Dell and Margery. "Do your show be instructive for the little ones? Do it be about sin and punishment?"

"Yes, of course. It's the story about the Children of Isreal fleeing from Egypt." Dell thought about the Children of Israel—how Egypt must have felt like a whole country of cannibals to them, with the cruel pharaoh doing everything he could to kill them.

Margery considered for a moment, then shook her finger at the children. "Sit," she commanded them. "All of you." They sat, their bodies forming a little half-circle in front of the stage.

"H-m-m-m-ph," Margery said to Dell. "I know what you needs. You needs a shouter." She glowered down at the five children. "If any of you moves a hair—any of you—I'll be boxing your ears until you cry for mercy." She set her basket of oysters in Matthew's lap, turned, and marched into the crowd. "Puppet show," she shouted. "Puppet show from across the sea! Today only! Hurry! Puppet show!"

The older juggler handed his fire stick to the boy and approached Dell. "See here," he said to her. "I be willing to take a risk on you. What say we be partners in business today? Our tricks be good at drawing the crowd, and your show—methinks—be good at holding them. And the money be jingling in the hat for us all."

Partners in business? Dell didn't know a thing about business, and the man standing before her was a stranger.

She looked out into the crowd. Margery was returning with a potential spectator on her arm. She had gotten him almost as far as the stage before he wrested free of her and stomped off.

Dell nodded at the juggler. "All right."

He smiled. "I be Hubert. And this be my boy, Valentine. And you?"

"Me? Dell. Odelia."

Margery picked up her basket and sniffed it. "I be done shouting. My oysters—and the little ones—they all be spoiling."

Valentine tossed the fire sticks to his father and somersaulted backward through the air. Dell scurried into the booth. She waited inside, peeking out now and then. Sure enough, a cluster of people was already forming around Hubert and Valentine.

The excited voices of children drifted into the booth. "Bartholomew," Dell whispered into his ear, "you are about to become famous." Bartholomew grinned from ear to ear.

And then another sound—the *clomp, clomp* of a horse—drowned out the childish voices. Dell held the puppets to her breast. She didn't breathe until the hoof beats were a distant echo.

In *The Flight Out of Egypt*, Bartholomew played Moses and Daisy played Miriam. Lucifer, of course, took the part of the wicked pharaoh. Dell had sewn a long purple robe to cover his tail, and she had fashioned a crown to hide his horns. All the puppets remembered their speeches, and even Daisy, who had been created only a week ago, acted with aplomb. Dell couldn't see the audience, of course, but she could hear them. They hissed when the pharaoh chased the Israelites, and they cheered when Moses parted the waters of the Red Sea.

When the puppets took their final bows, the booth nearly shook with applause. And when the clapping finally quieted, coins tinkled in Hubert's cap.

Dell and Hubert and Valentine worked together all afternoon, stopping only once to buy eel pasties from a passing vendor. Before she knew it, the sky was tinged with the dusty pink of twilight. Valentine snuffed out the fire sticks and laid down his cap. The Gypsy woman rolled up her rug. Was the day really ending so soon?

Hubert dumped out the coins they had earned and divided them into two equal piles. He pushed one toward Dell. "Fifty, fifty," he said. "We be a fine team."

"Thank you," Dell said. She picked up Bartholomew and folded his hands over his harlequin suit. "I'd say I was proud of you, but your head is already bursting with self-importance." She tucked him into the bag along with Daisy and Lucifer, pulled the string tight, then took the curtain rod down.

Church bells pealed, and she looked out over the dwindling crowd. Ronaldo would be at vespers now, she knew that, but her eyes scanned the square anyway. She took the stage apart and tied it together with the rope. Her arms ached from holding up the puppets, and her throat scratched from her loud singing and talking.

But Dell was happy. She had loved making her puppets come alive. She had loved the exclamations and applause of the crowd. And most remarkable of all—she had earned money doing it. She wondered if her mother had experienced the same joy and satisfaction when she'd held her puppets up to the stage. She would have to ask Ronaldo if he remembered.

She dragged the heavy stage into John's workshop and listened for the shuffle of feet upstairs or the clanging of pots and pans in the kitchen. "John?" She took out her coins, spread them across the work table, and counted them. Eleven in all.

On the way home, she had bought two warm buns, a chunk of cheese, and two tarts for their supper, and she still had money to spare. "John?"

A faint scraping sound came from the kitchen. A mouse, she hoped, not a rat. John was out again. He was often gone, usually all night. She was accustomed to his mysterious comings and goings, but right now she wanted him home so she could tell him about her afternoon.

She took Bartholomew out of the bag, set him on his pine stick, and carried him into the kitchen. "You, sir," she said, "will serve as my supper companion." Except for a few coals in the far corner, the fire was cold. And John had tracked his ashy footprints all across the floor. Or were there two sets? He hadn't cooked anything in the cauldron. He never cooked.

Dell raked the few hot coals forward. That scraping sound again. From inside the hearth.

Barholomew stood on the table, watching her. Images of bleating sheep and snarling wolves formed in her mind's eye. She leapt to her feet. "Fie on secrets and safety," she said to him. "Something's inside that hole and I will learn what it is."

CHAPTER

XXVI

Dell sat on her heels in the cinders. She wiggled one of the bricks loose and pulled it out. Her whole life had been nothing but secrets, and she was tired of them. She would find out what—besides the jug—lay hidden in the dark den inside the hearth. And if John came in and discovered her, well, all the better. She would demand an explanation.

She removed the bricks slowly, one by one, listening all the while for his footsteps. The dark opening grew wider and wider—a jagged, gaping mouth—and the pile of bricks at her side grew taller and taller. The dank smell drifted out and hung in the still air. Her hands grew black with soot.

Even though she had taken this sidewall apart once before, it was no less frightening this time. What if the sounds she'd heard were the rattling of dry bones? An ember crumbled into the ash, and she jerked upright. Or a meeting place for hobgoblins and ghosts? She pulled out another brick. No, it was probably just a secret storeroom for letters from the priests and monks. Just two or three more and the opening would be big enough for her to squeeze through.

A scratching sound caused her to pause. She held her breath and listened, but the blood pounded so loudly in her head that she couldn't tell where the sound came from.

She removed another brick, ever so quietly now, and then one more. She hitched up her skirt and inched forward on her hands and knees. Her head entered the den first, and a stale smell—one she didn't remember from before—filled her nose and mouth.

If only she had a lemon in her hand. She would breathe in its scent and feel renewed. Her heart beat faster, louder. She set one hand inside and then the other. Every muscle in her body was taut. She squeezed her shoulders together and forced them through the narrow opening. As her arms grazed the bricks, mortar crumbled onto her hands. She sucked in her breath. Paused. Inched forward.

The space felt close and stale—just like before—but something else, too—something that turned her skin to ice. She willed a trembling hand forward. Her fingers crept over the packed dirt. Farther, deeper. The jug. It was gone.

She crept forward, feeling for letters or quills. Maybe furniture parts. Her breasts, her backside, her legs, even her feet and toes were inside the black emptiness now. The darkness swallowed her, stifled her. She couldn't breathe. She bit down on her lip and tasted blood.

Breathing. Something else inside this tomb was breathing. Or someone else ... no, just her own fearful gasps.

A rustling sound. A shifting. The breathing. She had to get out of here. Now. She moved one leg back out through the jagged hole. She had to. ...

Claws dug into her wrist. "Let go!" she screamed. She

struck out with her free arm, but it only smashed against the wall. "Let go of me!"

A hand covered her mouth and pulled her close. She bit into the creature's flesh.

"Odelia," said a pained voice. "Peace, Odelia."

Dell went limp. "Brother Gregory," she gasped. "What? ..."

"S-h-h-h-h-h, child."

The monk's bony knees and elbows poked her, but she leaned against him and buried her face in his habit.

"I don't understand," she said, and then she lowered her voice to match Brother Gregory's whisper. "Why are you here?"

"I might ask you the same question." He sighed. "John built this keep for stubborn priests—those who won't sign the Oath of Allegiance." His head thumped as it struck the ceiling. "But—God help me—this dank hole is no place for a human soul."

"Come," she said. "I'll help you out." She took Brother Gregory's hand—the one she'd bitten—and guided him out into the kitchen. After she'd settled him at the trestle table, she poured two cups of ale and set one beside him. "You must be in grave danger to have shut yourself up in that—that tomb."

"John and Ronaldo persuaded me to hide in it until such a time as I might escape from the city. But you, child—you are at risk enough delivering the letters. You must not jeopardize yourself with further involvement."

Cromwell had seen her. He knew her name. She couldn't turn back now, even if she wanted to. In her mind's eye, she saw her mother being crushed by the rearing horse. "Lucretia resisted the king, and he killed her. I will not bow to such a man."

The shop door slammed shut and John marched into the kitchen. He stopped abruptly, as if he had walked into a wall. With one sweep of his eyes, he took in Dell and Brother Gregory and the pile of bricks. "God's wounds!" he shouted, then lowered his voice to a furious whisper. "What the devil is going on? If Cromwell and his henchmen come now, we'll be nothing but necks for their nooses."

"I am sorry, Odelia," Brother Gregory said. His arm bumped his mug and it fell over with a clunk. Ale ran across the table and dripped onto the floor. "I have put you at risk. I am like a man with pestilence who breaks quarantine and infects the living."

Dell grabbed a rag and mopped at the puddle of ale.

John glowered at Brother Gregory. "What are you doing out of the keep? Have you gone mad?"

Dell stood up, the rag dripping in her hand. "I took the wall apart. I am to blame."

"Nonsense," muttered the monk.

John opened his mouth then closed it. He wiped the sweat that had beaded on his brow. At last he took hold of Brother Gregory's elbow. "It's all right," he said gently. "Come along. I'll help you back in."

Brother Gregory's arm didn't bend, nor did the elderly

monk rise from his spot. He fingered the crucifix he wore about his neck. "When I took my vows, I did not promise to be faithful to any monarch or government. I swore to be faithful to the church and to God."

"Yes," said John, as if he was trying to calm an impossible child. "That's why you're here. Because you hold fast to your beliefs."

"As long as I cower and hide, I do not serve God's truth."

"Truth?" John said. His jaws clenched and unclenched, and then his voice regained its soothing quality. "The truth is—you haven't signed the oath, and you never will. If you don't escape, you will be killed, like the Carthusians. And a dead man can't serve God."

"Not true, my son. Think on St. Stephen, who was stoned to death, or on St. Peter, who was crucified upside down. Martyrs—by their deaths—inspire us weak members to stronger faith."

Dell sat on the edge of the bench, twisting the wet, sour rag. Everyone—except for her—seemed so certain they knew the truth. Ale dripped onto her shoes. Bartholomew stared straight ahead at the wall.

"You don't need to be dead to inspire others." John leaned close to Brother Gregory's ear. "Everything has been arranged. Tomorrow night—God willing—you will be gone from London and on your way to Kent. Come. Your stubbornness clouds your vision."

Brother Gregory held firmly to the cross. "My vision is clear."

Dell squeezed her hands around her throat until she couldn't swallow. Is this how the noose would feel? But hanging would be only the beginning. Next would come the stab of the knife into your belly and the sight of your own entrails held aloft. Dell thought of how Father had cut Ezekiel's belly open, how the rabbit had screamed in terror and agony.

Her back stiffened. "What about Ronaldo?" She didn't dare mention that Cromwell had also seen her at the monastery and had learned her name and followed her through the streets.

Brother Gregory waved his hand in the air. "I have ordered him to keep silent, and he has obeyed me."

"No," Dell said, her voice barely a whisper. "He has not. He defended you to Cromwell."

The monk's shoulder twitched slightly. "The boy will get a hiding for that."

"And that man—Cromwell—he threatened to write Ronaldo's name in his book."

Brother Gregory pressed the crucifix to his brow. "Christ, have mercy," he whispered.

Dell's throat felt strangled.

"I must return to the monastery." Brother Gregory pushed back the bench and rose to his feet. "I must see to Ronaldo. And I must take a stand for my beliefs."

John laid a hand on the monk's stooped shoulder and, with some effort, pushed him back down. "Cromwell's men could strike at any moment. Besides, it's nearly curfew. If the king's men don't imprison you in the Tower as a traitor, the watch will throw you in Newgate Jail as a nightwalker."

Brother Gregory turned his head toward the hearth. "If I crawl back inside that coward's cave, I am already a dead man."

Dell remembered what it had been like to live in their cave on the mountain. She could never return to that cramped, dim life. She thought of Ronaldo. What would he do when he learned that Brother Gregory refused to hide anymore? With whom would Ronaldo share his fears? She needed to talk with him. Now. She leapt to her feet. "Tomás ... he has a cart. ... I'll tell him Brother Gregory is ill and needs a ride."

"No!" John shouted. He slammed his fist on the table. "Brother Gregory must stay here." He glanced over his shoulder. "We cannot draw Tomás into this, too."

"We won't," Dell said. She grabbed her shawl off the hook, wrapped it around her head, and hurried toward the shop.

"Come back here," John commanded.

Before he could get to his feet, Dell had skirted around an oak chest and a broken stool. She was almost out the front door when a dull crash came from the kitchen. She stopped in alarm. Had the two men come to blows? She spun around.

There stood Brother Gregory, his long, misshapen body blocking the kitchen doorway, his gangly arms stretched from one side of it to the other. He must have been transported by angels to have moved so quickly. And where was John? She strained to see over the work table and its pile of boards. The poor man must have slipped in the ale and fallen to the floor.

Dell dashed outside and ran, trying to keep to the alleys and byways.

When she heard the heavy clopping of hoofs, terror seized her, and she shrank behind a butcher's stall. But then she thought of her mother—murdered by the king—and she came forward and ran with all her might.

XXVII

By the time she got to New Fish Street, she was out of breath, and her legs were weak as water. The Whitsunday festivities had ended. Margery's house was still and dark. *Please.* ...

From down the street came sounds of stifled laughter. At the corner stood Tomás's cart. He was leaning against it, and Margery was pressing close to him.

Dell felt a pang of jealousy. Margery was toying with both Tomás *and* Ronaldo and she didn't love either one of them. How could she!

"Margery!" Dell called out. "Tomás!"

Margery moved even closer to Tomás. "Go away," she barked. "You be shouting loud enough to raise the dead."

"And Margery's father as well." Tomás laughed and slipped his arm around Margery's middle.

"It's Brother Gregory," Dell said, panting. "He's ill. He was passing out bread near John's and fainted. He wants nothing but to return to the monastery, and he's too weak to walk." She nodded at the cart.

Tomás shrugged. "The monastery is on the way to Pembroke's Inn, where I'm lodged. And I should like to bid farewell to Ronaldo before I leave for home. Mayhap I can yet persuade him to sign the Oath of Allegiance."

Dell clutched at her shawl. So Ronaldo hadn't signed either. No, of course he hadn't. He would follow in Brother Gregory's footsteps.

Tomás untethered his horse and glanced up at the darkening sky. "We best hurry. It's nearly curfew."

Margery raised her chin and pushed out her bosom. She squinted at Dell, and her eyes sparked in challenge.

Tomás gave Margery an exaggerated bow. "When I return," he said, flourishing his cap, "I will bring you a ball of lavender soap. Adieu."

Margery curtsied in reply. "Adieu," she parroted. Her curtsey was clumsy, but it showed her bosoms to great advantage.

Tomás's horse plodded along, its spotted head bobbing up and down. Dell thought of Cromwell's huge horse, with its flaring nostrils and imperious gate. *Faster!* she wanted to shout, *Faster!*

When they finally arrived at John the Joiner's, Brother Gregory was sitting quietly at the table in the kitchen.

John was pacing back and forth. "I asked him to remain here for the night, but he insists on returning to the monastery."

Dell wrapped a blanket around Brother Gregory's shoulders.

John cast her a dark look, then turned to Tomás. "The illness has made him delirious, so pay no heed to what he says."

"I'm happy to be of service." Tomás took the monk's arm. "Come. Let me help you into the cart."

When the two men had left the kitchen, Dell grabbed John's sleeve. "I'm going with them," she whispered. "If I'm at Brother Gregory's side, and he's covered with a blanket, we will appear as father and daughter." And once they arrived at the monastery, she might see Ronaldo. She had to see him—maybe even feel the touch of his hand.

"If *I* were your father right now," John muttered, "I would beat you senseless."

"*You?*" Despite her panic, Dell smiled at the thought.

Dell ran outside. "I will accompany Brother Gregory," she said to Tomás. "He is weak and at risk of toppling from the cart."

"Suit yourself. But *you* will be at risk if you are on the streets after curfew."

"I have a friend near the monastery," she lied. "If the hour grows late."

They rode along in silence and made good time on the nearly deserted streets. The cart rocked and swayed, and Dell had to link her arm in Brother Gregory's to keep him upright.

"It was the best thing for him," Tomás said. He sat stiff-backed in the cart, staring straight ahead at the emptying streets. "Do you not agree?"

"Oh, yes," said Dell. "He will feel much better once he's back in his own bed."

Tomás clucked at the horse and continued to stare into the gathering darkness. "He was a mischievous pup," he went on, "always stirring up trouble of one kind or another."

A pup? Tomás wasn't talking about Brother Gregory. He was talking about Ronaldo.

"I couldn't make a place for myself in the world and watch after a lively boy like Ronaldo." Tomás leaned around Brother Gregory's hood, trying to see his face. "Brother Gregory?" All the arrogance had drained from Tomás's voice, and it had become almost pleading. "Ronaldo will make a fine Benedictine, will he not?"

Brother Gregory nodded slightly.

Tomás lowered his voice. "I have concerns for his mortal safety."

"Yes, my son, you have said so."

"I fear that your beliefs put him in extreme jeopardy."

Dell said nothing, but the skin on her neck prickled. What did Cromwell know of *her* involvement?

Brother Gregory's shoulder twitched against Dell's arm but his voice remained calm. "God's will is always done."

Was it really God's will that Brother Gregory and Ronaldo be tortured and hanged at Tyburn? And what about her? Would God will her to die with them? She drew the shawl around her shivering body.

Tomás drove the cart slowly until at last they came to the row of beggars that lined the monastery wall. They were silent, probably hoping to be ignored by the night watch. Ronaldo would be at compline, but still, Dell squinted into the gathering darkness.

Tomás steered the horse past the closed door and brought it to a stop alongside the monastery wall. He jumped from the cart and banged on the door. "Ho, there!" he shouted. "Ho, there!"

Dell held her breath and fixed her eyes on the door. Tomás banged again. The door opened a crack, and a cowled monk stuck out his head. Dell strained to see inside his hood.

"What is the cause of this disturbance?" the monk grumbled. Dell's heart sank. It was the voice of the scabby-headed monk. She squeezed her hands into fists. Evening had turned suddenly into night, and the darkness had swelled into a huge and hungry mouth.

"Brother Gregory is ill," Tomás announced. His voice was so commanding, Dell flinched.

The monk leaned around the door and peered in the direction of the cart. The instant he saw Brother Gregory's humped back, he sprang to attention. "Wait here," he said. "I am too feeble to be of service, but I will fetch someone who can help." Leaving the door ajar, he hurried off.

"I best go," Dell said, trying to hide the disappointment in her voice.

Tomás paced by the cart. "Adieu," he mumbled.

Brother Gregory patted her knotted hands. "Godspeed." She hopped down from the cart. She *would* need the speed of God to get home before curfew.

But instead of running, she crept past the monastery door, then along the row of beggars. The little mute girl raised her arm in a crooked greeting.

Even if Dell did make it back home before curfew,

she would find herself in a cold and empty house. John wouldn't be there—he never slept at home anymore, and Bartholomew—well, Bartholomew would be some comfort. But tonight she needed more than a cheeky puppet. She needed to talk to someone who would understand her fears—someone who might hold her hand in his. She looked back over her shoulder at the open door of the monastery.

Outside the door, alongside the wall, stood the cart. Tomás paced back and forth beside it, and Brother Gregory sat patiently on its narrow seat, his back to Dell. She turned and inched her way along the wall. Voices whispered for alms.

Could Tomás hear her? She couldn't see him clearly in the dark, but his pacing footsteps continued in the same clipped rhythm. Her chest was tight, her senses sharp. She moved silently toward the door until she stood between it and the beggar girl.

Tomás's horse whinnied.

"Gadzooks," Tomás complained. "We've waited long enough." His dark figure hopped up into the cart. "Come, my good man. I'll carry you inside myself."

Dell sucked in her breath. She had to see Ronaldo. She stuck her head inside the open doorway. From the monastery grounds came the *thump, thump* of footsteps. Someone—Brother Gregory's helper—was coming. In an instant Tomás would enter the grounds, too. Dell flung herself through the open gate.

The footsteps grew louder. To her left was the dark

bulk of a hedge. She dove behind it. The monk was moving rapidly toward her.

Dell could make out the frame of his body, the unmistakable rhythm of his gait. Of course. The older monk had fetched Ronaldo. In another moment he would pass by her. She leaned into the hedge. "P-s-s-s-s-t," she whispered.

Ronaldo stopped. "Hallo?"

"It's Dell ... Odelia."

"Odelia? What?" Ronaldo ran to the hedge and tried to force his way through the shrubbery. "Where's Brother Gregory? Is he all right?"

"Yes," she whispered. "But I took apart the keep and found him, and he knows that Cromwell threatened to write your name, and he won't hide anymore, and Tomás brought him—"

"Stay here," Ronaldo said. "I'll be back." Before she could reply, he had disappeared into the darkness.

She crouched low, listening for Ronaldo and Brother Gregory. It wasn't long until they shuffled by. Neither of them spoke. Contrary to Ronaldo's orders, Dell followed along in the shadows.

When they stopped and disappeared into the largest of the stone structures, Dell stopped, too. She sat under a tree and hugged her knees to her chest. The grooved bark pressed into her back. Above her stretched the sky—an enormous, endless sky—almost like the one on the mountain. It was all black, except for a sprinkle of stars and a slender white moon.

On the mountain she had waited for that same moon to appear so she could run down to the fallen fir tree. She remembered how she had crouched behind the tree with Bartholomew, hoping for lemons, longing for the Boy. And now here she was, under the same moon, waiting for the same Boy. But everything else was different. She was in the City of Cannibals now. And she was a part of it.

In a way, Father had told her the truth. The city was rife with cruelty. But here in the city she'd talked to the Brown Boy and learned about her past. She'd seen to it that Bartholomew had become an actor and she a puppeteer. She'd become a part of something dangerous, something that mattered.

But if she hadn't taken the hearth apart, Brother Gregory would be safe inside the keep. What would happen to him now? And what about Ronaldo? What about her? Burning eyes seemed to glint in the darkness. Hungry jaws snapped.

After a long while footsteps thudded past her, and she leapt to her feet. "Here," she whispered. "I'm here."

CHAPTER

XXVIII

Ronaldo hurried to her side. Without a word, he took her hand and led her across the dark monastery grounds into a secluded ring of pine trees. The trees rose around them, a circle of silent sentinels.

"Sit," he said, and pulled her down into the cushion of pine needles. "We're safe here. Tell me all."

"You must know about the secret keep at John's?"

"Of course. I delivered Brother Gregory to it."

"He says he won't go back. He says he will remain here and stand up for the truth."

Ronaldo snatched up a large stick and cracked it against a tree.

Dell winced.

"I won't leave him. I can't." A shudder passed through his body. "And in any case, if my name is in Cromwell's book. ..." He bowed his head. "I am a coward." His body trembled as if he were crying. "I don't want to die."

"Nor do I." Dell reached out a hand to touch him, then withdrew it. So, their souls were of one accord in this matter.

But surely no one, no matter how cruel—not even a cannibal—would torture such a frail and gentle man as

Brother Gregory. No one would hang a young man just for being loyal to his aged teacher, would they? And what of a girl who would not swear allegiance to a king who had murdered her mother?

Ronaldo's heaving body was answer enough.

Oh, no, no, no. This was all wrong. A hideous mistake. God would never allow such a thing. Never.

Ronaldo raised himself and wiped his eyes with the sleeve of his habit. Even in the dark, Dell could see a corner of the harlequin fabric he had stitched inside. A tear hovered on the rim of his eye, then ran in a crooked path down his cheek.

She felt as powerless as the beggar girl. Nothing could alter the course of events set in motion by a mighty king. She reached out a trembling finger to his face and caught the tear in its path. She wanted to tell him that he needn't be ashamed—who wouldn't cry in the face of death? "Ronaldo—"

He pushed himself to his knees and reached out to her. He cupped her chin in his hand and raised her face to his.

She jerked her head sideways. "Don't!" she choked. "It's not right."

Ronaldo rose and turned his back to her. His shoulders rose and fell with his labored breathing. "In these days, nothing is right."

"I need to go." She felt hollow inside, and her words dropped into her own emptiness, clinking like coins in a tin cup. She ran her hands down her skirt, smoothing it over and over.

The galloping hoof beats of the white horse pounded in her head. There must be some way to make that huge beast leave them alone. There must be some way to return to that dewy moment when Ronaldo's hand first touched hers, some way to go back to a time when she was still ignorant and safe from all this hate and love.

"Can't someone stop him?" she asked. What a stupid question. No one could stop a king.

Ronaldo pounded the tree with his fist. "Thomas More tried. He was a courageous man, a man of fine words. Even a friend to the king."

"And?"

He drew his thumb, like a knife, across his throat. "His head rolled a fortnight after John Fisher's."

Dell flinched. Fisher—the frail old man who had been beheaded her very first day in the city.

"And now six monks have been hanged until almost dead, then disemboweled at Tyburn. Twelve shackled and starved to death at Newgate Prison." Ronaldo dropped to his knees. "I can't leave Brother Gregory."

Dell nodded dumbly. "Of course not," she said. "Nor can you be false to the truth."

Ronaldo lifted his head. "The truth? It is not the truth I desire. What I covet is my brother's life."

Dell's body gave a little jolt. Of course Ronaldo wanted Tomás's life—it included Margery. What a simpleton she'd been. She remembered now the way Ronaldo and Margery had teased together, how he had admired the sway of her womanly hips. Ronaldo loved Margery, but Tomás would be the one to have her. Ronaldo was jealous of his brother. Something inside Dell crumpled.

"Not his wealth," Ronaldo went on. "I care little for worldly gain. It is his freedom I covet." He reached out for Dell's hand, but she withdrew it.

Ronaldo *wasn't* talking about Margery. He was talking about freedom. She knelt beside him.

"I have no confessor to whom I can say this." He reached for her hand again and grasped it so tightly it throbbed. "I don't ... I'm not ... my thoughts and desires ... oh, God, have mercy ... my prayers are a mockery ... my Latin ... I am nothing but a common boy."

"You must take heart," Dell said. "In time your mind will become pure like Brother Gregory's."

"In time?" Ronaldo cried. "Don't you understand? *I haven't any time.*"

Dell's gut churned. Losing Ronaldo to Margery or to God had been a crushing thought, but losing him to torture and death. ...

For an instant Father's face—hard and contorted—flashed before her. The anguish he must have felt when Lucretia died! And the anger! How had he continued, day after lonely day, convinced that he had failed her? "Surely there's something—couldn't you talk Brother Gregory into escaping the city—the country—he could be a monk some-where else—in your homeland—you could go home. ..."

"I have made every argument to convince him. I thought

I had saved him—*us*—when I delivered him to John's keep. We were to leave the city tonight, under the cover of darkness."

Dell's gut swirled. If she had left the bricks in place, if she hadn't interfered, Brother Gregory and Ronaldo would be on their way to safety and life. "But you couldn't have left by night," she said, desperate to be exonerated. "The gates close at curfew."

"Aldersgate has an underground passage—for those traveling after curfew. And that clothing you delivered last Sabbath—the skirt and apprentice suit?" He pushed aside a pile of pine needles and pulled out the bundle. "Our disguises."

Dell shivered so violently, Ronaldo removed his cloak and laid it over her shoulders. "I'm sorry," he said. "What of you?"

"Me?" Should she tell him how Cromwell had followed her through the streets that day? How he had come to her puppet shows, watching, listening?

"I mean—how will you get home now? It's long past curfew."

Dell shrugged. Getting home. A trite matter compared to the troubles that loomed ahead. She nodded toward the big stone building. "You should go. Brother Gregory will be looking for you at compline."

Ronaldo shook his head. "Tomás said Brother Gregory must be kept in the infirmary tonight." He managed a weak smile. "That frail body of his is stronger than it looks. Why—he'll probably live to be—" Ronaldo let out a moan.

Dell reached out and brushed her fingertip over his. It was a sin to touch him like this, but it seemed now a small transgression compared to the monstrous evil galloping toward them.

She couldn't alter the course of the great white horse. It would come—it *was* coming. But it had not trampled them. Not yet. They still had this unmeasured moment, this holy place. Tonight she still had the chance to give him a small token—a farthing—of her love.

She touched the tips of his fingers, one by one, willing her own meager strength to flow into his, to rush through his veins and flood him with fortitude for the trials ahead. A strange animal sound escaped from his lips, and Dell pulled back, frightened. She needed to go. Now.

But if she could just feel the warmth of his skin one more time—just once more—it would give her the strength she needed to leave. She knelt beside him, reached out, touched his chin. She moved her finger across the stipple on his jaw. The strange roughness startled her, awakened her the same way that the sour taste of the lemon had. Ronaldo's chest rose and fell, but his hands remained motionless at his sides. A quivering sensation—a sliver of liquid lightning— shot through her.

She leaned over him and pressed her cheek against the coarse warmth of his habit. His heart was pounding loud enough to wake the entire monastery. Or was it her own?

"It's all right," she whispered. "Everything's all right." It was a lie, of course. Or was it? Maybe for this one fleeting moment everything *was* all right. She and the Boy were here together in a fragrant bed of pine. Around them the vigilant trees stood watch. If only she could hold on to this moment, make it last forever.

He lifted her face to his, but she turned away. His breath came shallow and ragged. "Come," he said with some effort. "I'll walk you home."

She turned back to him, and his eyes met hers. The fear and sorrow on his face stung her with anguish. She wanted him to be happy again, to be the smiling Brown Boy who had sat in the patch of sunlight beside the sack on the mountain.

If she hadn't meddled in his affairs, he might still have a chance for happiness and life. She raised her face and— before she knew it—brushed her lips over his.

A violent shudder convulsed Ronaldo's body, and Dell drew back, ashamed. What vile thing had she done, touching the lips of a monk?

But Ronaldo didn't move away. He grabbed her face in his hands and kissed her so fiercely she cried out.

"Forgive me," he choked. He drew back but continued to grip her face in his hands. He stroked her cheek with the back of his hand, then drew his trembling finger over her lips. He kissed her again, more gently now, and yet again, until at last her frozen lips parted, and she kissed him back. A torrent of need flooded her. Her skin tingled. She fed him kiss after kiss, and he fed her, but their kisses only made her—them—ravenous for more.

And then the word *whore* erupted inside of her, and she pushed herself away.

Ronaldo gasped for breath. "Odelia," he said. "Don't go. Stay with me this night."

"I can't." Dell knew from the Bible that lying with a man who was not your husband was a grievous sin. "In the eyes of God, I would be defiled." And yet how could she leave him here alone in this hour of trial? She pressed his fingers to her lips. "Maybe God, in His mercy, will close His eyes."

Ronaldo drew her close. "Odelia," he whispered. "I love you."

Ronaldo slept with his head on her breast, his body twitching beside her. What was she doing? What delusions—what devils?—had led her to this? The boughs of the pines drooped over her, blotting out the moon and the stars. *Maybe God, in his mercy, will close His eyes.* Ha! God never closed his eyes. Carefully, slowly, she wrested herself from under Ronaldo's arm. A moan escaped from his lips. "Odelia," he mumbled.

Dell shivered. She would never answer to that lovely name again. She was Dell, plain Dell. A stupid, sullied girl. Nothing more.

The night was still black as pitch, but somewhere a cock crowed. She remembered the story of Peter in the

Bible—how the night before Jesus was crucified, he had denied his Lord thrice before the cock had crowed twice. Hadn't she—with her sinful actions—denied her Lord, too? How could she claim to know and love God and commit this abomination?

Whore. She had allowed the devil to twist her mind into believing that kissing a monk and sleeping at his side—his head on her breast—were godly acts.

Before the cock had crowed once, she had denied her Savior. She had done it stealthily, as if the darkness could hide her sin. But no matter how obscure the night, God had seen them. He had witnessed their coming together, heard their labored breathing.

Soon the cock would crow again. It would condemn her as she lay defiled in the bosom of a man who belonged to God. She fumbled for her shawl. She had sinned once—she could never undo that—but she would not succumb again.

This had been her doing. She had touched his lips. She had been the temptress, the Eve. She leapt up and ran for the gate, stumbling over the lumpy sod, falling to her knees, rising again. She ran out the monastery gates into the street, almost hoping the night watch would throw her into prison where she belonged.

She ran along the deserted streets. She skirted around shadowy forms in doorways and ducked into alleys when the cry of the night watch came close. Sharp needles of pain stung her side. A cackling sound—like the laugh of the crippled beggar woman—filled the dark sky.

Dell clapped her hands over her ears. "Leave me alone," she cried. But the sound came again, jagged and piercing. Oh, God have mercy—it was a rooster, proclaiming the possibility of a bright new day. She leaned against a wall, hugging herself, allowing the tears to course down her cheeks.

For her, this day and every day to come would dawn stained and dirty. She could not undo what she had done. The darkness was dissolving, and she would have to look at herself in the glaring light of day. Her body heaved with sobs. The city was waking. Nearby a lock clicked, a shutter creaked.

CHAPTER

XXIX

A fortnight had passed since Whitsunday, the night of her sin. Heavy with shame, Dell continued at her daily activities. She cooked and cleaned for John, and she presented puppet plays alongside Hubert and Valentine. Sometimes another man—one as finely clad as Cromwell, but with a pocked face—would stop to watch her puppets and listen to their words. After the shows he would linger, talking in low tones to Hubert and Valentine. But Hubert would only shake his head at the man, and Valentine would shrug his shoulders.

Most evenings now John slipped out before curfew and didn't return until dawn. He never admitted where he had gone, but the dark half-moons under his eyes told enough. He was such a master of disguise. Every morning he would wash his face and shave it smooth. Then he would tie on his apron and stride, humming, into his shop—a simple, merry joiner.

Dell wore a disguise now, too. A mask of innocence. She went about her daily chores as if she were still an untouched maiden, ignorant of men. Only she and Ronaldo—and God, of course—knew the real Dell—the temptress, the Eve.

She prayed that she was not with child. She wasn't

ignorant. She'd seen how rabbits and goats conceived, but men and women—might it not go more delicately? Mary, the mother of God, had borne Jesus, and she was a virgin. Dell fasted on Wednesdays and Fridays in penance, but also with the hope that an unborn child—if there was one—would fly away if it found nothing to eat in her womb.

Margery would know the signs, but Dell couldn't ask *her*. She could already see Margery's hands on her hips, her thrust-up chin. "You *do* be a whore!" she would crow in triumph. No, Dell would have to bear this burden alone.

And yet … some deep, aching part of Dell *wanted* to bear Ronaldo's child. She yearned for his babe to swell in her womb, to suckle her breasts. Then, at least—if she wasn't hanged at Tyburn—she would still have Ronaldo's child after he was dead.

Dead. Her belly knotted. In a way, he was already dead—to her at least. If he ever looked at her again, he would do it with contempt, the way the scabby-headed monk had stared at her. If only she could go back to the time before she had kissed him and laid her body down beside his.

She continued to deliver letters to the Carthusian monks and to the Grey Friars, but never to Ronaldo's monastery. It was too late for that. Brother Gregory had decided to stand up for his beliefs, and no power on Earth could dissuade him.

Once she saw Ronaldo outside St. Sepulchre, giving bread to a blind man. He laid his hand with such tenderness on the man's head, Dell prickled with jealousy. *She* wanted to be the one receiving his gentle touch. She pulled her shawl over her head and hurried home.

The shop was empty except for Bartholomew. She slipped him on her hand. "I have sinned against God," she said. "I have lain with Ronaldo."

"For money?"

Dell smacked him on the head.

"I thought not." Bartholomew rubbed the injured spot. "Well, then. Do you love him?"

"You, of all people, should know *that*."

He laid his mitted hand on hers. "And is love a sin?"

"Why must you always ask the prickly question?" She jerked her hand out from under his. "All right. If you must have an answer, then yes, love is a sin."

Bartholomew made the sign of the cross. "Then God preserve us."

Before he could utter another word, Dell yanked him off her hand and jammed him on his stick.

The next morning, while she waited in the bakery queue, the women's talk was more excited than usual. Dell caught bits of their conversation. *A grand wedding procession. A four-hundred-gun salute. Wine running in the conduits.*

"The new queen will bear him a son," said one. "You'll see."

Another lowered her voice. "I say Jane Seymour is

already carrying the king's child. Else why would he marry her so soon?"

"Quite so," added a toothless woman. "It's been but three weeks since he sent that whore—Anne Boleyn—to the block." Her voice dropped to a whisper. "I heard she took an unborn child with her to the scaffold."

The other women clucked their reproaches, but Dell kept silent. What if the same fate befell her? Something twisted inside her, and she clutched at her belly. But then she passed wind and the knot in her gut disappeared.

She made a new puppet—a girl with downcast eyes and thin, straight lips. Dell named her Dolores, for the puppet's countenance was dark with sorrow. Dell positioned her hand in Dolores's costume in such a way that the belly of it bulged out, making it appear that the puppet was great with child. "Shame on you," Dell said. "Shame."

One morning John appeared at breakfast with a rare smile on his face. "Wednesday next is the twenty-fourth day of June," he announced. "You must polish your stage."

Dell looked at him dumbly.

"It's Midsummer's Eve. A great festival day."

"Like Whitsunday?"

"Whitsunday is but a pale shadow of Midsummer's Eve. Everyone will be reveling. There will be a parade and explosions. It will be a fine opportunity for you and your puppets."

But less than a week away! Dell set to work with great industry, if not joy. Joy had fled on the night of her sin. Bartholomew suggested they perform a new miracle play—the story of Adam and Eve. A good choice. Dell knew all about Eve. Bartholomew would be Adam, and Daisy would be Eve. Lucifer would play himself, of course, and Dolores—she would be the angel who would drive Adam and Eve from the Garden of Eden with a flaming sword.

But Dell wanted something new in this performance. Something startling that would attract the crowds. Hubert and Valentine always drew a fine audience, but she yearned for something of her own creation.

She paced back and forth in the shop. Bartholomew was no help. He believed that he was attraction enough. What about a picture to go with her new performance? She thought of the church window the soldier had shattered—the picture of Adam and Eve in the Garden of Eden. Eden—so lush and abundant—so different from what people saw in this dim and dirty city.

The Garden would be a perfect backdrop. If she could make it unique and colorful, people would come close to see it and stay for the show. She'd never painted a picture before, but she *had* painted the faces of her puppets, and even strangers had praised their lifelike features. She nailed the fabric to the wall, pulling it tight.

Where to begin? She drew a peacock, like one she had seen in the square—its tail open like a lady's fan—and then a rabbit with the same brown and white markings as Ezekiel.

She left a space for the tree—she would add that last. She drew a monkey and a wooly sheep, and stepped back from her work. Her drawings were good—much better than she had imagined they would be.

But something was lacking. She stepped close to the painting, and the charcoal in her hand seemed to move, of its own accord, over the fabric. What was she drawing? A dog? No, a wolf. A wolf in the Garden of Eden!

She painted the creatures, and while the paint dried, she straightened the shop. She wished John were here to see her painting, but he had borrowed Tomás's cart and was out delivering completed projects to his customers. Or so he said. She turned to Bartholomew. "Well," she said. "What do you think so far?" Bartholomew's expression indicated that he was of two minds. The picture was pleasant enough—so long as it didn't detract from *him*.

She picked up a brush. Now for the tree. The Tree of Knowledge of Good and Evil. She had seen the tree depicted in stained glass windows and in Auntie's Bible as well. It was an apple tree, she knew that much, and the forbidden fruit a bright red apple. She painted a sturdy brown trunk and then leafy branches that spread out over all the creatures in the garden. The tree looked lush and inviting, if she did say so herself.

When the paint had dried, she picked up her charcoal and drew an apple on a low-hanging branch. But something was wrong with that apple. It wasn't round. It had the shape of an egg, with nubs on both ends. She stepped closer. Why, it wasn't an apple at all. It was a lemon. A *lemon* on the Tree of Knowledge of Good and Evil. Who ever heard of such a thing?

Still. A lemon had brought her close to the Boy and had awakened memories of her mother. A lemon had refreshed and soothed her. It had helped heal Margery's brother. How could a lemon be the forbidden fruit?

That day on the mountain she'd dug into the sack, frantic to find one. And having tasted it, she'd wanted more. More of the sour flavor, more of the grinning Brown Boy, more of the whole, succulent world. Confused, she turned to Bartholomew.

"Was it all sinful?" she asked. "Was coming here—was everything—sinful?"

"Ah," said Bartholomew. "What does a squash know of sin?" He gave a wry smile. "As for me, I am glad we came to the City of Cannibals. Here I have become what I was created to be. My puppet booth is the best home I could wish for."

Dell returned to the backdrop. She had to admit that she loved working inside the booth as much as Bartholomew did. And surely it was no sin to help people forget—for a few brief moments—the harsh tedium of their lives.

She painted another lemon on a higher branch. Then another and another. She filled the entire tree with lemons— bright yellow lemons—so many, the branches must bend with their weight—and when the tree was full and ripe and bursting with fruit, she stepped back, and no matter if her audiences might *Tsk! Tsk!* at the idea of lemons growing on the Tree of Knowledge of Good and Evil, she looked at the tree and the animals and the vines and flowers—she looked at the whole lush Garden and saw that it was good.

XXX

On the morning of Midsummer's Eve, Dell rose at first light, thinking of Brother Gregory and Ronaldo. "Preserve them from the jaws of the Wolf," she prayed. But even as she knelt in prayer, she was also filled with an eagerness for her new puppet show. For shame. How could she feel delight while Brother Gregory and Ronaldo—and maybe even she—lived in the midst of so much danger? How could grief and joy live side by side within a single heart?

She prepared the breakfast pottage and waited for John to return from his meeting, or wherever it was he went at night. Shortly after dawn the door creaked open.

"Good morrow," Dell called. John didn't answer. He strode through the workshop and into the kitchen, thumping his fist in his palm. His cap was pulled almost low enough to hide his red eyes and the dark half-moons beneath them. "John?"

He picked up his shaving knife, then threw it on the table. Dell jumped out of his way.

Other mornings he always entered the house in a matter-of-fact way. In the blink of an eye, he could exchange his secret nighttime self for his cheery John-the-Joiner self. But this morning he seemed unable to trade one mask for the other.

He picked up his shaving knife again but cut himself just below his lip. He cursed and paced the kitchen, a crooked thread of blood trickling down his chin.

Dell chewed her lip. "John?" She offered him a rag to wipe the blood, but he seemed not to notice. "I kept the pottage warm for you."

He stopped and looked at her in surprise. "Pottage, you say? No, it is too late for pottage."

Too late. Dell's gut cramped, but it was not due to any unborn babe. "Is there anything to be done?"

"Done!" he cried. "Done!" He slammed his fist on the table then collapsed on the bench and buried his face in his hands.

Dell packed up her stage and puppets and headed for the square. She trudged along Dowgate Street then turned onto Thames. She plodded up Garlick Hill as if her ankles were locked in iron manacles. As she walked, she listened for hoof beats. A breeze came up, lifting her skirt and blowing dust in her eyes.

She went to her usual spot, a stone's throw from the door of St. Paul's. Hubert and Valentine were already there and had held a space for her. She set down her load, and together they set up her booth.

"Keep an eye on your stage," Valentine said. "A west wind be throwing sparks willy-nilly." He crooked his arm and showed Dell the burn hole on his sleeve. He glanced uneasily at the backdrop. "That wolf in your picture. It be looking right at me."

Hubert studied the painting, too. "Well," he said at last, "I never be seeing yellow apples before, but they catches the eye, they do."

Something tugged at the hem of Dell's skirt. "Alms," said a whining voice. Dell whirled around. There at her feet was the crippled beggar woman—*again*. Anger rose in Dell, and she fought the urge to scream at the sickening sight. The stiff breeze blew the woman's stench right in Dell's face. Like always, the beggar's dirt-encrusted hand was extended. "For a farthing," she croaked, "I will pray for you."

"I don't need your prayers," Dell snapped.

The woman rocked back and forth and her tangled ropes of hair swung with each awkward jerk of her body. "Adam and Eve and apples and Eve," she chanted in a sing-song voice. "Apples and apples and Adam and Eve."

Dell recoiled. Did the woman know that Dell—like Eve—had tempted Ronaldo and led him into sin? Furious, Dell gave the woman a shove with her foot. She toppled over onto her back and lay there, cackling up at the gray sky.

Dell thought of how Brother Gregory had reached out to the beggar girl and laid his hand on her grimy hair. Dell's face grew hot with shame. How could she be so cruel— kicking a woman who had nothing—no home, no money, no legs? She should ask the woman's forgiveness, but her stench. ...

Hubert took hold of Dell's skirt and pulled her back. "Easy now," he said. "She be nothing but a pitiable old woman."

Valentine pulled the woman upright and dropped a farthing in her hand. She bit down on the coin and dropped it in her pouch. Then she dragged her body close to the stage and sat in front of it, rocking and chanting, "Apples and apples and apples and Eve." The woman was going to stay and watch Dell's show. How dare she!

Hubert seemed to read Dell's thoughts. "Leave her be," he said.

"Her stench will drive people away."

Valentine covered his mouth and nose with his hand and nodded in agreement. His voice came out muffled. "Her hairs got more creatures crawling in it than do the Garden of Eden."

"Enough," Hubert growled. "Both of you." He fastened his floppy cap and set the juggling sticks in a small brazier to catch fire.

Dell laid out her puppets inside the booth—Daisy on her left side and Bartholomew on her right. Lucifer, in his black, serpentine costume, lay on the far side of Bartholomew. And Dolores, a little wooden sword tied to her hand, lay next to Daisy.

Dell weighted the backdrop curtain with stones so the wind wouldn't jostle it. There. Usually, inside her sturdy booth, she felt safe. Invisible. She couldn't see out and no one else could see in. But today a wooden booth was no fortress against the approaching evils.

Valentine thumped twice on the side wall—their signal that a crowd was gathering. Just as Dell slipped Bartholomew on her hand, a puff of wind riffled the curtain. With a whoosh, the breeze swirled into the booth and blew down her neck. Dell's skin prickled. Another presence hovered behind her. An evil spirit? She spun around.

There stood Jennet. "I come back," she said. She pointed at Lucifer. "Bad."

From outside the booth came the sounds of Margery's frantic cries. Dell led Jennet to the front of the booth, where Margery stood, surrounded by her four brothers.

"Jennet," Margery said. "Shame." She yanked Jennet close and gave her a smack on her ear. "Sit," she commanded. "All of you."

Three of the boys grudgingly obeyed, but Ned drew back, pointing at the beggar woman. "She stinks."

Margery crinkled her nose. "She do indeed." She pushed the boys to their feet and herded all five children to the right of the stage. "Sit here then. It be upwind."

As the children settled themselves, Valentine executed a series of somersaults, and Hubert stomped out a few remaining sparks. When a goodly crowd had gathered, Dell nodded at Hubert and hurried back into the booth. Lucifer lay on his back, grinning wickedly at her. Hadn't she turned him facedown, as she had the other puppets? A puff of air tickled her neck again, and again she shivered. She turned Lucifer over, then slipped Bartholomew on her right hand and Daisy on her left.

The show went well. When Bartholomew was talking, she felt as if she were Adam, and when Daisy spoke, she became Eve. When she slipped her hand into the long, black body of Lucifer, a sense of evil rose inside her.

While her puppets spoke their lines, her ears remained attuned—as always—to the noises of the crowd—their cheers and hisses and exclamations. But today she was listening for something more—the hoof beats of the great white horse.

The performance was nearly over. Adam and Eve had tasted the forbidden fruit and could never return to their life of innocence.

The angel—Dolores—stood in front of the Tree of Knowledge of Good and Evil, brandishing her sword. "Go!" she commanded. "Because you have eaten of the tree, your sorrows will be multiplied." A knowing murmur went up from the crowd.

But another sound, too. A clomping sound. Maybe it was the beggar woman rapping her stick on the booth.

"For dust thou art," the angel went on.

Dell's gut tightened. The clomping sound had become a clatter.

The angel's voice rose shrilly. "And unto dust thou shalt return."

The hoof beats were coming this way.

XXXI

"The end," Dell shouted. She yanked the puppet down from the stage. The audience cheered, but even their noisy applause could not drown out the steady *clomp, clomp* of the horse's hooves.

She flung Dolores to the ground and grabbed Bartholomew. "What am I to do?" she choked. She pulled him on her hand and shook him. "Answer me!"

"The wolf is come for the sheep."

"I know," she cried. She peeked out from the booth—across the square—over the heads of the crowd. "Cromwell—he's tethered his horse and dismounted."

Bartholomew shuddered. "He has watched me perform before, that viper-eyed devil. He mingles with the audience and listens for seditious speeches."

"Today he will ride on to the monastery." Dell wiped away the beads of sweat gathering above her lip. She thought of her mother, crouched inside her puppet booth. Had she known the king's soldier was coming for her? Had she felt this powerless and afraid?

"How long will you cringe in this booth?" Bartholomew cried.

"Stupid puppet! What do you expect I should do?"

Dell leapt to her feet. Maybe there *was* something she could do. She and her puppets. She could move them about on the stage. She could give them voice. If she created a powerful enough distraction, she might divert Cromwell. Could a puppet show engage—*or enrage*—him enough to make him forget his mission?

Frantic, she dug through her bag of costumes until she found the ones from *The Flight out of Egypt*. Yes—here the pharoah's golden crown ... here his purple robe.

Her hands trembled so violently, she could barely jam the crown onto Bartholomew's head or fasten the robe about his neck. She wriggled her free hand into Lucifer's costume. This man of the king might kill her for this performance, but he wouldn't crush her.

She leaned around the side of the booth. The audience still lingered, no doubt hoping for another performance. And in the midst of them, Cromwell.

She raised Bartholomew and Lucifer up to the stage. When the audience had quieted, Bartholomew lifted his head and spread his arms wide. "Look at this great land around us," he said in his loudest voice. "And tell me, Lucifer—am I not a mighty monarch?"

Lucifer bowed before him. "The mightiest of all."

"Long live the king!" a voice in the audience shouted.

"Am I not the manliest in the hunt and surest in the joust?" said Bartholomew.

"Without compare, your majesty."

"Long live the king!" the crowd called out in one voice.

"And have I not the fairest maidens in my bed chamber?"

Lucifer coughed. The audience grew silent.

"Ah, your majesty," Lucifer said. "The fairest maiden has escaped the palace with a dwarf."

"Disperse!" a voice bellowed outside the booth. "Every man! Disperse if you value your lives!" Gasps and cries rose from the crowd.

Dell yanked her puppets down from the stage. Hugging Bartholomew to her breast, she peered out. Cromwell had grabbed Hubert by his collar and was shaking him. Then he gave Hubert a shove and marched through the crowd to get to his horse. Only the beggar woman remained, rocking and muttering.

Bartholomew's eyes were wide with alarm. "Well, now you've done it."

"*You* goaded me," she retorted. "But I'm glad—I'm *glad* I won't go to my grave in silence." She thrust him into her pocket.

In a moment Cromwell would return for her—and march on to the monastery. She had to get to Brother Gregory and Ronaldo. If she could just warn them ... tell them that the Wolf was on his way ... surely they would choose to escape. Maybe they could all escape together. She pulled Lucifer off her hand and flung him to the ground.

"P-s-s-s-t."

Dell turned, startled. Hubert and Valentine huddled on the other side of the booth. Valentine motioned to her with his fire stick. "You must go with haste. When he returns, we'll tell him you be heading for the bridge."

"But what of *you?*"

"We have hidey-holes. Now go!"

Valentine pushed on her leg, urging her on.

How could Ronaldo and Brother Gregory escape unnoticed? Dell's mind swirled. The disguises. Tomás's cart. She pushed her way into the crowd, stumbling over the beggar woman. Margery and her brood were heading toward a pie man.

"Margery!" Dell shouted. All six heads turned her way. "Margery—can you drive Tomás's cart?"

"Do you be mad?"

Dell rushed to Margery and grabbed her shoulders. "When he sailed for home, he left it at your house, did he not?"

Margery wrenched herself from Dell's grasp and twisted a lock of hair around her finger. "Tomás be showing me how to drive it," she said coyly. "But it aren't a womanly accomplishment."

"You must bring it to the monastery. *Now.*"

"I might be doing it ... if you tell me the benefits."
Margery crossed her arms and planted her feet.

By Heaven! If this mulish girl wouldn't move of her own accord. ...

Dell turned to the little ones. "Children," she said. Her gaze darted between them and the approaching Cromwell. "Run home as fast as your legs will go, and I will buy each of you your very own sweet cake." She glanced at Margery. "And one for your sister, too."

Luke gave a whoop, and they all took off across the crowded square.

"Come back!" Margery cried. "All of you!" She picked up her skirts and ran after them as fast as she could.

"The cart!" Dell shouted. "Bring the cart to the monastery."

Across the square, the horse had begun to move this way. Its hoof beats pounded inside Dell's head.

Should she throw herself in front of Cromwell? Beg for mercy?

No. The Wolf had no mercy. And Bartholomew's speech about a lecherous king had enraged Cromwell.

From behind her came the familiar cackle—and stench—of the beggar woman. "Apples and apples and Adam and Eve."

Dell spun around. Valentine was hopping about the woman, stamping out sparks from his fire stick.

Fire. *That* might slow the Wolf. Dell crouched beside Valentine. "The stick. I need your stick." She grabbed it from his hand and dashed into the booth.

"Come, boy," Hubert called. "We be no match for these troubles."

Dell thrust Bartholomew into one pocket and Daisy into the other. Her hands shook, but she held the stick to a corner of her painting until the flame caught. It spread delicately at first, nibbling at the tail of the monkey, the wooly legs of the lamb, the underbelly of the wolf.

Maybe she *was* mad, like the beggar woman. This booth was all she had. She looked out—into the crowd. The face of the Wolf bobbed along, above the sea of people.

She turned back to her painting. The whole garden was melting now—the leaves and flowers and lemons. This was her livelihood—the sky-blue curtain, the walls with their dovetail joints, the tree lush with lemons.

A puff of wind swirled into the booth and the flames leapt higher—farther—until the backdrop was a wall of rippling flame. She brushed off the sparks that fell on her shoulders and thought of her mother, trapped in a booth like this one, the horse rearing up.

Dell flung down the stick and ran. She fought the urge to turn and look back. Even now the flames would be dancing along the stage, creeping up the curtain and the walls of the booth. In a moment Lucifer would catch fire, and Dolores. She glanced over her shoulder. Sparks danced in the wind and the ashy shreds of the backdrop swirled upward. Her eyes stung with smoke. The wind teased the flames into a frenzy. She pushed on through the crowd.

Someone screamed.

Cries of *Fire! Fire!* rose from the crowd.

There was a loud crackling and then a smashing sound. Women screamed, men shouted, children cried. What had she done? A fat butcher waddled past her, water splashing out of his pail. The screaming and shouting drowned out the sound of hoof beats. Had Cromwell gone away? She squinted over her shoulder into the smoke.

Cromwell's rigid back, his jowly cheeks were coming this way. He snapped the reins, but his horse shimmied sideways. No creature was foolish enough to walk across a bed of fire.

She had gained a few moments, maybe enough to reach Brother Gregory and Ronaldo. Smoke billowed so thick, she could barely see Cromwell anymore. He would never be able to spot her. Not yet. Coughing and choking, she fought her way through the panicked crowd. The hoof beats pounded in her head, spurred her on.

It seemed hours before the walls of the monastery rose before her. When she arrived at the gate, she threw herself on it, pounding and screaming. The beggar girl withdrew into her blanket.

The scabby-headed monk cracked open the gate. His eyes sparked with anger, but Dell shoved him aside. "He's coming for them," she gasped. "For Brother Gregory and Ronaldo. I've got to warn them."

The monk made the sign of the cross. "In the garden," he said, "back of the pines."

Dell ran along the hedge and through the circle of pines where she and Ronaldo had lain together. In the needles lay the bundle of disguises. Shame and guilt choked her. Would Brother Gregory and Ronaldo listen to her? Would Ronaldo regard her as nothing but a debased woman?

She spotted them behind a small stone building. The boy was on his hands and knees pulling weeds, and the aged monk was stooped over a furrow, loosening the earth with a hoe.

Dell waved her arms wildly. "Ronaldo!" she shouted. "Brother Gregory!" The elder monk planted his hoe upright in the earth, and Ronaldo rose to his feet. Dell longed to rush into his strong arms, but instead she ran to Brother Gregory and clung to his habit.

Brother Gregory took her hands and held her at arm's length. "What is it, child? You smell of smoke."

Ronaldo stood, unmoving. From his hand hung a gnarly weed.

"He's coming," Dell choked. "The Wolf ... Cromwell ... Margery's coming ... I hope ... with the cart." She tugged on Brother Gregory's sleeve, but he seemed rooted in the earth. Ronaldo stood silent at his side.

"I thought he might choose this day," the monk said. "The whole city is merry and drunk with ale."

Frantic, she fell at Brother Gregory's feet, clasping his ankle. "Please," she begged. "We haven't much time."

Ronaldo threw aside the weed and pulled Dell to her feet. The dirt that encrusted his hand made it feel dry and crumbly, but his grasp was firm. He looked at her not with the contempt she expected, but with tenderness. "Brother Gregory and I will stay," he said. He took hold of her elbow. "Come, I'll walk you to the gate. You're not safe here with us."

She pulled her arm away. "I'm not safe out there either. Bartholomew ... that is ... I ... spoke out in the presence of Cromwell. Against the king."

Ronaldo wiped the sweat from his brow. "You spoke out for the Pope? For the church?"

Dell pulled on her tangled strands of hair. "No. I ... I ... spoke out for my mother ... for myself. I can't explain."

"You mean *you* are in danger also?" He turned and faced his mentor. "Brother Gregory. We must see to Odelia's safety."

"My son," said the elder monk, "it is your duty to obey me in all things, is it not?"

"Yes, Brother. I'll follow you wherever you go. But please—you heard what Odelia said."

"Patience, my son." Brother Gregory jabbed the hoe into the furrow, and the blade made a crunching sound as it sank into the dry earth. He drew in his breath and let it out slowly, as if he had all the time in the world. "It is your duty to *obey* me, not to *follow* me. You are not a slavish dog, but a boy—a man—with a soul. As a novice, you have made great efforts."

Stop your talking! Dell wanted to scream. *Cromwell will be here any minute!*

Ronaldo shifted from foot to foot.

"But," Brother Gregory continued, "your heart is not in your vocation."

Ronaldo's face paled. The elderly monk spoke the truth. Ronaldo had said the very same thing. That night under the pines he'd told her how he coveted Tomás's freedom.

"Therefore," continued Brother Gregory, "I have advised the abbot that you are not called to the monastic life. He has released you from this order. You must go."

Dell let out a gasp. Brother Gregory was trying to save Ronaldo's life. But if they didn't stop talking. ...

"I will go to the scaffold with you," Ronaldo said. "God will give us the courage we need in our hour of trial."

Brother Gregory held fast to his hoe. "Where I go," he said, "I will need but a brief moment of strength. But where *you* go will require a lifetime of courage. More than I possess."

Dell bit down on her knuckles. Why did any of them have to die? Why couldn't God come down right now and transport all of them directly into Heaven? Where *was* God?

Brother Gregory fumbled for her hand, then for Ronaldo's, and brought their soiled palms together in between his. "Love God by loving one another. Now go. Immediately."

Ronaldo stared at Dell with dull eyes. "Cromwell is come for you also?" he repeated. "You also?"

"I do not want you," Brother Gregory said to Ronaldo, his voice fierce.

Dell's legs shook. The Wolf would be here any moment. If only she could persuade Ronaldo to come away with her. But she had tempted him into disobedience once and she wouldn't do it again. This time, he would have to decide for himself.

"You *will* obey me!" said Brother Gregory. He raised the hoe and held it over his head like a pike.

"Don't!" Dell shouted.

She dropped to her knees just as the hoe sliced through the air. Ronaldo threw himself on Dell, and the heavy tool skimmed over him. The elder monk swung the hoe again, so wildly now it smashed against Dell's shoulder and she cried out.

"I have decided," Ronaldo said.

Before they could scramble out of the way, the hoe came down again, and Ronaldo screamed. Two of his fingers bloomed red. He looked at his bleeding hand as if it belonged to someone else.

Brother Gregory made the sign of the cross. "Christ have mercy on our souls." He turned and shuffled away, leaning on his hoe for support. Dell helped Ronaldo to his feet.

They stumbled along until they reached the circle of pines. Dell gathered the bundle of clothing while Ronaldo meandered toward the gate. As he walked, blood dripped to the ground. His face was pale, his expression void. "Your hand," she said, when she caught up to him. "Hold it up, near your chest."

Ronaldo obeyed, lifting his arm as if it were a weed from the garden.

Dell yanked Bartholomew from her pocket and ripped the suit from his head. As she bound Ronaldo's hand with the harlequin costume, the boy stared, unflinching, at the monastery wall ahead of them. Dell picked up the bundle and thrust it toward him. "Here," she said. "You must exchange your clothing. Quickly."

When he made no attempt to take the bundle, she untied it and shook out the contents. She snatched the flask and coins off the ground, leaving the other items—

the blue apprentice shirt and leggings—for Ronaldo. She should exchange her clothing, too, but her fingers trembled so hard, she couldn't unlace her bodice. "Hurry!" she cried. "The Wolf!"

The throbbing in her head was so loud now, it sounded as if it was pounding both inside her and outside her at the same time. Maybe it was. Maybe the white horse was at the monastery gate right now.

She grabbed Ronaldo's arms. What was the matter with him? Had he changed his mind already? "You must exchange your clothing," she said. "Unless you desire to remain here with Brother Gregory."

Ronaldo slowly unbelted his habit, and Dell turned away so he would not feel ashamed at his nakedness.

XXXII

When she slipped outside the monastery door, Cromwell
—the Wolf—wasn't there. But Margery—praise be to
God!—had come with the cart. She stood beside it, clutching
the horse's reins and chewing on the string of her cap. She
shook her finger at Dell. "It aren't proper for a lady to be
driving a cart, you know. People be looking. It aren't right."

Dell glanced up and down the street. No white horse.
Not yet. "Thank you for coming."

"You *should* be thanking me. And what of the sweets
for the little ones?"

Just then Ronaldo stepped out from the gate. His
bandage—Bartholomew's suit—was soaked with blood.
Margery stared, wide-eyed, at the blue apprentice suit and
the bloody wrap. "Do this be some Midsummer Eve prank?"
She twisted her cap string around her finger. "Where be the
old monk?"

"He—he couldn't come," Dell said. "He sent us on."

"The two of you?" Margery said shrilly. "Alone?" She
scrambled onto the seat. "Something be amiss—I smells
it." She gripped the reins with both hands. "But I aren't
asking questions—just get in the cart, the both of you—
no—I aren't asking no questions at all."

Dell and Ronaldo clambered up beside her. "You need only take us as far as Aldersgate," Dell said.

"Aldersgate? By Heaven!" The wet cap string dropped out of her mouth. "You be leaving the city then?" She clucked at the horse and the cart lurched forward. The little beggar girl raised her crooked arm as they passed by, but no one returned her salute.

As they bumped along Bladder Street, a sound from behind the cart made Dell's back go rigid. Hoof beats. She did not turn to look at the horse or the rider. Ronaldo's lips moved, but no sound escaped from them.

"I aren't asking questions," Margery said again, "but what do I be telling Tomás when he be returning with my lavender soap and my velvet ribbon? If you do not be here in the city?" With her elbow, she pointed at Ronaldo's bandaged hand. "What do I be telling Tomás about that bloody stain?"

"Tell him that his brother is safe," Dell said, hoping that she was telling the truth. "Thanks to your pluck."

"H-m-m-p-h." Margery grunted. She pushed out her bosoms and gave the reins a snap.

Dell had presumed the cart would move quickly through the city, but the streets were crowded, and it seemed like hours before they reached Fenchurch Street. Margery—rather deftly—steered the horse around several fallen drunks, a group of morris dancers, and a noisy parade led by a huge dragon. The Midsummer's Eve revelers paid no heed to the plodding cart.

Margery glanced sideways at Ronaldo's hand. "You be hearing about the fire today—in the square?"

Dell bit her lip. "I saw the smoke."

"They be stopping it before it got to the streets—only one be dead."

Dell's chest tightened. "Someone died in the fire?"

"Only that stench-full beggar woman. She be trampled in the crowd."

Dell slumped over. Why had she kicked that poor, helpless woman? Had Cromwell begun the same way—committing small acts of malice? Was she responsible for the woman's death? What if her soul were cultivating seeds of meanness that would grow into strangling vines of evil?

No. She would never allow those seeds to sprout and grow. She would nurture instead the seeds of compassion. She would tend her soul so it could blossom into a beautiful garden. Dell clenched her jaw and set her eyes on the street ahead.

Margery stopped the cart twice—once to fill their flask with ale, and once to buy bread and three eel pies. Margery set one pie in Ronaldo's lap, but he seemed not to notice it. Dell took a bite of hers, but it caught in her throat when she tried to swallow.

Margery ate her portion, then licked her fingers. "You be needing food and drink—if you be going somewhere—though I not be asking where you be going."

Dell looked to Ronaldo, but his face remained expressionless. Where *were* they going?

"Tomás—when he returns—he be having questions, you know."

Dell kept an eye on Ronaldo's hand. The harlequin bandage had turned bright red.

"Well," Margery announced, "here you be." She tugged on the reins and the horse came to a halt. The gates of the city rose before them. Revelers poured in and out, laughing and pushing and kissing. A minstrel played his lute. A monkey did somersaults in the air. Today the whole city was exuberant and expansive.

And yet ... Father had told her the truth. This *was* the City of Cannibals. This *was* a place where people devoured one other. And now she, too, was a part of it. She had been cruel to a helpless woman. Dell reached into her pocket and clutched Bartholomew's disembodied head. Nothing would ever be the same again.

The sweet scent of cinnamon and cloves caused Dell to turn her head. A woman near the gate was selling gingerbread husbands. Dell took three pennies from her pocket and pressed them into Margery's hand. "Please," she said, "You must buy five husbands—one for each of the little ones. I promised them."

Margery stuck out her lower lip. "And what of me? What of *my* labors?"

"Six, then."

Margery wrapped her arms around Dell and kissed her wetly on the lips. Flustered, Dell climbed out of the cart, and Ronaldo clambered down after her. He stumbled into a one-eyed goat—*a penny a touch*—then righted himself and headed into a group of swaggering soldiers. Dell hurried to his side and slipped her arm in his.

"You best be coming back soon." Margery pushed the string of her cap back into her mouth and chewed furiously on it. "Tomás—he be bringing even more lemons next time—do you hear—*a whole crate of lemons.*"

Dell steered Ronaldo through the crowd, looking back every few moments, straining for a glimpse of Margery. When Dell reached the gate, she turned.

High above the crowd rose Margery's face. She must be standing—balancing—on the seat of the cart. She waved her cap, and Dell waved back—tears stinging her eyes. This was a City of Cannibals, but it was something more as well.

Margery cupped her hands around her mouth. "Adooo!" she shouted over the noise of the street. Then her face took on a sudden look of surprise—and dropped out of sight. Dell guessed what had happened. In her eagerness to bid them farewell, Margery had lost her footing and toppled into the cart.

"Adieu," Dell murmured. With Ronaldo's arm in hers, she pushed her way through the city gates.

The road outside the city was well-trafficked. Carts rattled, goats bleated, children shouted. Ronaldo stumbled and fell, but the other travelers paid little heed. Everyone seemed to have goods to deliver, people to meet, places to go.

Dell invented a story, just in case someone questioned them. "You are a joiner's apprentice," she explained to Ronaldo, "and I am your sister. We're going to visit our mother in the city of—" Of what? The only city *she* knew was the City of Cannibals. And she dared not ask advice of other travelers, for fear of drawing attention.

Ronaldo trudged forward, plodding through his unreachable world of pain and sorrow. All right, then. She would decide for them both. Besides the city, there was only one destination she knew. If they cut off the road and walked all night, they could get to Auntie's cottage by dawn. Auntie—with her knowledge of herbs and remedies—would know what to do for Ronaldo.

But Ronaldo's pace slackened with every passing hour. Grief hung like a millstone about his neck. At dusk they stopped under a sycamore tree to rest, and Dell unbound his hand. It had swollen and felt warm to the touch. When she washed his fingers with ale from the flask, he winced from the pain, but didn't raise his eyes. It seemed as if the evils of the city had followed them out the gates and were pursuing them, even now.

Bartholomew's costume was heavy with blood, so Dell took Daisy from her pocket, ripped off her gown, and made it into a fresh wrap. Ronaldo's cheeks were flushed. Before she'd finished wrapping his hand, his head slumped over.

Ronaldo had chosen to come away with her. But what if he now regretted leaving Brother Gregory? What if he hated her for tempting him away? Above them the moon rose, sharp and slender as a scythe.

If they could make it to the cottage, Auntie would make a poultice for his hand and a medicine for his sickness. But what if Ronaldo's malady rose from a wounded heart? What if there was no remedy for such an affliction?

Sometime near dawn, Ronaldo awoke with a groan. Despite the morning chill, he was sweating. They drank the last of the ale and walked toward the mountain. In truth, the mountain was only a hill—she'd learned that from Ronaldo. But this morning a mountain lay before her.

XXXIII

Slowly they began their ascent. Dell remembered how Ronaldo had once sauntered up the path, bouncing along as if the sack were a bag of feathers. How different he looked today, his shoulders slumped, his gait unsteady. And what of the smile he'd once worn on his face? What of the cheerful spirit that had radiated from him?

They plodded along. A lark sang, the mist dissolved, and a startled hare bounded across their path. At this pace, they would still be walking when night fell.

Dell draped Ronaldo's good arm over her shoulder and encouraged him upward, step by step. *Come now, just to that big rock ... that's right ... only a few more steps to the hickory tree ... can you hear the stream? That's it, just a hundred paces more ... we'll count ... one ... two ... three. ...*

They were near Lucretia's wooden cross when Ronaldo leaned his back against a tree and slid to the ground. "Ronaldo," Dell said. "We're but halfway there. You must get up. For Brother Gregory's sake."

Ronaldo's hand lay limp in his lap and his eyes stared at—at nothing.

After all these trials, he was leaving her. A spark of resentment flared in her. How dare he? And then a wave of compassion—and shame for her anger—washed over her. "Christ have mercy," she prayed.

Before she could say *amen*, a pinecone struck her squarely between the eyes.

"I *said*, WHAT HO? Are you deaf and dumb?"

Dell jerked back her head. There sat her brother, straddling the fallen pine tree. He had tossed an empty sack over the trunk and was sitting astride it as if he were atop a fine horse.

"Nathaniel?" She stared at him, open-mouthed. "What are you doing here?" And then she remembered. Last night the moon had waned to its slenderest self. Nathaniel was waiting for the Boy to come with his sack. How small and innocent he looked up there, compared to the sight of Cromwell astride his great white horse.

Nathaniel threw another pinecone—hard—at Ronaldo. "Who's *that*?" The pinecone hit Ronaldo's shoulder and bounced to the ground.

"He's the monk—the novice—the boy—who brings the sacks up the mountain. And we need to get him to Auntie. Quickly. He may be—he's badly injured."

Nathaniel's gaze roamed up and down the blue apprentice suit. "A monk?" He spat. "No monk came at the last waning. Father sent me, but no one came."

"These have been trying times for the monks," Dell said. She glanced at Ronaldo. "I'll explain later." If only Nathaniel were taller, he could support Ronaldo as they walked, or carry him on his back.

Sack in hand, Nathaniel slid off the tree and loped toward them. How long had it been since she'd seen that cocky swagger of his? Could it really have been only two phases of the moon? She wanted to kneel and draw him close, but he would only shove her away. For Nathaniel, an embrace would be a sign of weakness.

Dell ran to the stream and filled the flask. She held it to Ronaldo's lips and—praise be to God—he drank.

"Move aside," Nathaniel said. He pushed at her with his boot. "This is man's work." He laid the empty sack on the ground, and with a good deal of huffing and puffing, hauled Ronaldo onto it. Then Nathaniel took hold of the two front corners of the sack, pulled them over his shoulders, and with a grunt, heaved his load forward. Dell walked at his side, grateful to have a companion who could talk to her.

"Did the cannibals try to kill him?' Nathaniel asked. "Was there a battle?"

Dell thought back over the last days and weeks. "Yes, there was a battle."

Nathaniel licked his lips. "I want to go with you. To the city. I'm not afraid."

"I could take you to a shop that sells only swords."

"Nothing but swords?" Nathaniel's eyes widened, and he pulled himself up as tall as his short body would allow.

She glanced over her shoulder, where Ronaldo slumped on the makeshift sled. "We'll go back soon ... when Ronaldo's stronger ... if ... when it's safe."

Nathaniel pressed close to her side. "I told Father I

would go to the city. He came at me with a stick, but I'm too quick for him now. I'm too strong." He paused to catch his breath. "He calls out your name in his sleep, you know, and Auntie—she prays for you when she thinks I'm not about."

"Father and Auntie—they could come, too."

Nathaniel laughed. "Father curses the city, and Auntie says that it's more wicked than Sodom and Gomorrah." He licked the sweat off his lip. "Is it?"

"Yes ... that is ... no." She thought of the people—the *friends*—she'd left behind. Hubert and Valentine, who'd always saved a place for her on the square and had split their earnings with her. And John, who'd given her a home and a puppet stage. What if Cromwell knew of *John's* involvement? Dell shuddered. And of course Margery. Oh, how she wished Margery were at her side right now, smelling of dead fish and calling her a ninny. "We must keep walking. I'll tell you all later."

The day grew hotter, and Nathaniel's pace slowed. As he plodded up the path, his chatter ceased. Despite his manly zeal, he was spent. Dell insisted that they stop, and she and Nathaniel shared the bread from her pocket.

"Nathaniel," Dell said. "Run ahead and—" She stopped in mid-sentence. Nathaniel would never willingly obey her, unless she bribed or flattered him. "You are stronger and fleeter of foot than I. Run ahead. Tell Auntie to make a poultice for Ronaldo's hand and a caudle for him to drink."

"Is he—you know—touched in the head? Or only deaf and mute?"

Dell tried to keep her voice calm. "If you take the message to Auntie, I'll buy a new sheath for your dagger. In the city."

Nathaniel chewed on his bread. "*Auntie* will never obey *me*."

He was right. But surely Auntie had once known Brother Gregory. And Auntie, like Lucretia, must have experienced his compassion. "Tell her that Ronaldo, the novice overseen by Brother Gregory, needs her help."

Nathaniel shrugged. "I suppose I've nothing better to do." He picked up the empty sack, threw it over his shoulder, and headed up the path.

"Tell Auntie we haven't come to stay," Dell called after him. "Tell Father, too."

Dell kneeled beside Ronaldo, but his eyes were so dull, it seemed as if his spirit had already slipped away. What if he died right here, so close to her mother's grave? She shook him, but he only gave a little moan. Could nothing restore him to life?

Desperate, she pulled Bartholomew's head from her pocket and fitted it on her pointing finger. The puppet stood before them, naked as a newborn babe.

"H-m-m-m-p-h." Bartholomew looked down at his bare skin, then raised his chin proudly. "A great actor can perform without a costume."

"But today—this is no performance."

"I understand." Bartholomew cleared his throat and crowed—*cock-a-doodle-doo*. Then he hopped up and down and waved his arms in Ronaldo's face.

Nothing.

"A stubborn case," Bartholomew muttered. Then, all of a sudden, he grabbed the Boy's nose and tweaked it as hard as he could.

Ronaldo startled, and a faint light sparked in his eyes.

"Pay heed to me, young man," Bartholomew commanded. "I am about to sing."

Ronaldo looked up and down Bartholomew's unclothed body. A smile flickered on his lips. "So you would perform naked, would you, you naughty man?"

Bartholomew spread his arms wide. "Hey, nonny, nonny," he sang out. "Hey, nonny, nonny no."

Dell's hand trembled, and a tear ran down her cheek. Bartholomew—unashamed—sang even louder. And painfully off-key.

Ronaldo pushed himself to his knees, then rose unsteadily to his feet. "I will walk," he said, "if it will stop the torment of his singing." He pushed back his shoulders and gazed up at the cloudless sky.

He looked comely in that blue apprentice suit—far more handsome than he had in his black habit. Dell remembered the pleasure with which he'd picked up John's hammer and awl. "That suit fits you well," she said. "As if it were made for you."

He looked down at his blue tunic in surprise, as if he'd never seen it before. "Mayhap it was."

Dell tried not to engage him in further conversation. He was weak, and he needed all his strength to walk. But so many questions bubbled inside her. "Are you sorry you left Brother Gregory?" she blurted out.

Ronaldo paused, too weak to walk and talk at the same time. "I told you—I have never shared in the purity of his convictions. I was staying out of loyalty."

"Yes, yes, I know. But do you want to go back to him? Do you despise me for tempting you away?"

Ronaldo frowned. "The decision was a terrible one to make, but it was mine alone. I chose to be with you."

"But ... what about that night ... don't you despise me for my ... for our. ..." Dell's face grew hot with shame. "For our sin?"

Ronaldo reached for her free hand. His swayed slightly but his eyes met hers. "Odelia," he said. "My love for you was—*is*—no sin."

Dell's mouth went dry with disbelief. He loved her? Even now? She needed to stop talking to him so he could concentrate on walking, but her tongue would not keep silent. "What will we do? Where will we go?" She held the puppet head to her breast. "And what of Bartholomew. I can't abandon him."

"Of course not." He wiped the sweat from his brow. "Brother Gregory was a grave threat to the king. But you and I—if we stay in remoter towns a while—I think the king will forget us."

"My stage and curtain, two of my puppets—they are all destroyed."

"Those things can be made again. Your *talents* have

not been destroyed. They live inside. ..." Ronaldo's words trailed off, and his hand felt sweaty in hers.

Why had she persisted in chattering when he was so weak? "S-h-h-h-h," she said, giving his hand a squeeze. "Save your strength. We can talk later."

Later. The word rang out like a chiming bell. It heralded a fresh tomorrow ... a brand new season ... an entire lifetime.

Then Brother's Gregory's face flashed in her mind's eye, and the joyful chiming clanged like a death knoll. *Later.* It was what the faithful monk no longer had.

Nearby the stream burbled, a robin trilled, and the first shadows of late afternoon fell across the path. Dell had one more thing to say that couldn't wait until later.

"I love you," she whispered.

"Oh, pish," said Bartholomew.

But Ronaldo held fast to Dell's hand, and together they continued up the mountain.

AUTHOR'S NOTE

City of Cannibals takes place in England in 1536. Although most of the characters who inhabit this story are fictional, the world in which they live is real.

In 1527 Henry VIII had been married to Catherine of Aragon for eighteen years. When their marriage failed to produce a male heir, Henry blamed Catherine and demanded that the Pope grant him an annulment so he could marry Anne Boleyn. The Pope refused, so Henry broke ties with the Roman Catholic Church and set himself up as head of the church in England. In 1533 he married Anne, and she became queen.

In order to gain complete control of the English church (and all its wealth and power), Henry shut down over eight hundred monasteries and convents and took them over for his personal use. Seven thousand monks and nuns willingly left their posts, but some refused, maintaining their loyalty to the Roman Catholic Church and to the Pope.

John Fisher, the elderly bishop whose execution Dell witnesses, was beheaded in 1535, not 1536, as the story suggests. Sir Thomas More, who is also mentioned in the story, was beheaded in the same year.

Thomas Cromwell was also an historical figure. Minister to Henry VIII, he headed up a group of men called the *visitors* or the *inquisitors*, who went from monastery to monastery, interrogating the priests and, depending on how they responded to Cromwell's questions, charging them with treason. Cromwell actually carried a little black book in which he recorded the names of those he considered guilty of treason. Between 1535-1539, over thirty monks were executed for treason, often after being tortured.

Most of the monks executed were Carthusian, a hermetic order of the London Charterhouse. Seven Benedictine priests were executed, but unlike Brother Gregory, they did not live in London. Although Westminster Abbey, in London, was Benedictine, it had political ties to the government and upheld the king's authority.

There is no record of a royal soldier crushing a former lady-in-waiting under a puppet booth. But we do know that Henry VIII had many lovers, and that he beheaded Anne Boleyn and Catherine Howard, two of his six wives. So although the event in the story is fictitious, I believe it could have happened.

This period of history and the human beings who created it are vastly more complicated than my brief summary suggests. If you want to learn more about the people and events in this story, you can find a wealth of fascinating information about this period.

ACKNOWLEDGMENTS

The act of writing is a solitary endeavor. The process of becoming a writer, however, often requires not isolation, but community. I'm deeply grateful to the people who have nurtured and supported me on my journey: the Muskrats and Jane Resh Thomas, our brilliant and beloved mentor; Deborah Keenan, gifted poet and teacher; my colleagues at Vermont College, and especially my advisors, Marion Dane Bauer, Louise Hawes, Norma Fox Mazer, and Phyllis Root; my insightful editor, Joy Neaves; Kaethe, Michael, and Agnes, who make me laugh; and Peter, who always says *yes*.